Perhaps he was married...

The thought was an unwelcome one which Margo thrust aside. Why shouldn't he be married with a brood of children? It was none of her business. She did want to know, however. Margo being Margo, it was no sooner said than done.

"Are you married?" she asked him. Then regretted it the moment she had spoken; the look of amused surprise on Gijs's face sent the color into her cheeks and she mumbled, "Sorry. That was rude of me...."

"No, I'm not married." He ignored the mumble. "I have never found the time."

Betty Neels spent her childhood and youth in Devonshire, England, before training as a nurse and midwife. She was an army nursing sister during the war, married a Dutchman and subsequently lived in Holland for fourteen years. She lives with her husband in Dorset, and has a daughter and grandson. Her hobbies are reading, animals, old buildings and writing. Betty started to write on retirement from nursing, incited by a lady in a library bemoaning the lack of romantic novels.

Books by Betty Neels

HARLEQUIN ROMANCE®
3483—THE MISTLETOE KISS
3492—MARRYING MARY
3512—A KISS FOR JULIE

$\mathscr{B}$etty Neels

The Vicar's Daughter

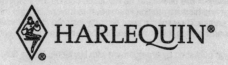

HARLEQUIN®

TORONTO • NEW YORK • LONDON
AMSTERDAM • PARIS • SYDNEY • HAMBURG
STOCKHOLM • ATHENS • TOKYO • MILAN • MADRID
PRAGUE • WARSAW • BUDAPEST • AUCKLAND

ISBN 0-373-3527-6

THE VICAR'S DAUGHTER

First North American Publication 1998.

Copyright © 1996 by Betty Neels.

CHAPTER ONE

IT WAS a crisp, starry October night and Professor van Kessel, driving himself back home after a weekend with friends in Dorset, had chosen to take the country roads rather than the direct route to London. He drove without haste, enjoying the dark quiet, the villages tucked in the hollows between the hills, the long stretches of silent road, the unexpected curves and sudden windings up and down. There was no one about, though from time to time he slowed for a fox or a badger, a hedgehog or a startled rabbit.

The last village had been some miles back and now there were no houses by the roadside. It was farmland, and the farmhouses lay well back from the road; there would be another village presently and he could take his direction from there. In the meantime he was content; the weekend had been very pleasant and this was a delightfully peaceful way of ending it.

The road curved between heavy undergrowth and trees, and he slowed and then braked hard as a figure darted from the side of the road into his headlights, only yards from the Rolls's bonnet. The doctor swore softly and let down his window.

'That was a silly thing to do,' he observed mildly to the anxious face peering at him, and he got out of the car. 'In trouble?'

The girl stared up at him looming over her small person. Her face might be anxious but there was no sign of distress or fear.

'Hope I didn't startle you,' she said, 'and so sorry to

5

bother you, but would you stop at Thinbottom village—
it's only a couple of miles down the road—and get
someone to phone for a doctor or an ambulance?
There's a party of travellers in the woods—' She
cocked her neat head sideways over a shoulder. 'One
of them is having a baby and I'm not sure what to do
next.'

A plain face, the doctor reflected, but lovely eyes and
a delightful voice. What she was doing here in the middle of nowhere at eleven o'clock at night was none of
his business, and considering the circumstances she was
remarkably self-possessed. He said now, 'Perhaps I
might help. I'm a doctor.'

'Oh, splendid.' She gave his sleeve an urgent tug.
'Have you got your bag with you? We'll need scissors
and some string or something, and a few towels.
There's a kettle of hot water...' She was leading the
way along a narrow track. 'I told her not to push...'

The darkness hid his smile.

'You are a nurse?'

'Me? Gracious me, no. First aid. Here we are.'

The travellers had set up their camp in a clearing
close to the path, with a tent, a small stove, a few bundles and a hand-cart.

'In the tent,' said the girl, and gave his sleeve another
urgent tug. 'He's a doctor,' she said to the two young
women, and to the man and young boy standing there.
'Did you lock your car?' she asked the doctor. 'Because
if you didn't Willy can go and stand guard over it.'

'I locked it.' What a little busybody the girl was—
probably some vicar's daughter. 'I'll have a basin of
that water in the tent. With a towel, if there is one.'

He bent his large frame and edged inside, and a moment later the girl crept in with a saucepan of water
and a none too clean towel to make herself small on

the other side of the woman, waiting to be told what to do.

The doctor had taken off his jacket and rolled up his shirtsleeves. 'Something in which to wrap the infant?' He smiled reassuringly at the woman lying on top of a sleeping bag. 'You're very brave—another few minutes and you'll have your baby to hold.'

The woman let out a squawk. 'It's early,' she mumbled. 'We'd reckoned we'd be in Sturminster Newton.'

The doctor was arranging some plastic sheeting just so, and getting things from his bag set out on it. He glanced over at the girl. 'A blanket? Something warm?'

He whipped a spotless and very large handkerchief from a pocket as she took off the scarf wound round her neck and, urged on by the imminent arrival of the baby, she laid the one on the other just in time to receive a furiously angry infant.

'You'll have to hold her for a moment, then wrap her up tightly and give her to her mum. Right, now do as I say...'

He was quick and unflurried, telling her what to do in a quiet voice, making little jokes with the mother. Presently he said, 'Go outside and see if anyone has a clean towel or nightie—but they must be clean.'

She crawled out of the tent, and with the other women's help searched the bundles.

She came back with a cotton nightie. 'This one was being saved for when she got to Sturminster Newton.'

'Excellent. Roll it up neatly and give it to me.' In a moment he said, 'Now, put your hand just here and keep it steady while I phone.'

He took a phone from his pocket and dialled 999 and began to speak.

He went outside then, and presently the husband came in to bend awkwardly over his wife and daughter while the girl knelt awkwardly, cold and cramped, her hand stiff.

The father went away and the doctor came back, took her hand away gently and nodded his satisfaction. 'The ambulance will be here very shortly; they'll take you to Blandford Hospital—just for a couple of days so that you can rest a bit and get to know the baby. Have you any transport?'

'Broke down yesterday.'

He went away again to talk to the husband, and came back with two mugs of tea. He handed one to the girl and helped his patient to sit up, and held the mug while she drank. 'If I might suggest it,' he said in his placid voice, 'it would be a good idea if your husband and family stayed for a day or two in Blandford. I think that I may be able to arrange that for you—it will give you time to sort things out. You'll be quite free to go on your way, but you do need a good rest for a couple of days.'

'If Bert don't mind...' The woman closed her eyes and slept, the baby clasped close to her, its cross little face now smoothed into that of a small cherub.

The doctor glanced across at the girl, still kneeling patiently. She was smiling down at the baby, and when she smiled she wasn't in the least plain. When she looked up he saw how pale she was. 'Are you not out rather late?' he asked.

'Well, it was just after seven o'clock when Bert stopped me. I was on my way home on my bike, you know. There's not much traffic along here after five o'clock. Two cars went by and he tried to stop them, but they took no notice...'

'So you had a go?'

She nodded. 'She'll be quite comfortable at Blandford—but it's a bit late...'

'I'll go in and see whoever's on duty at the hospital.' He sounded so reassuring that she said no more, and they crouched, the pair of them, beside the woman, saying nothing. From time to time the doctor saw to his patient, and once or twice he went to talk to her husband. He was packing up their possessions and stowing them on the hand-cart. When the doctor returned the second time he told the girl that the boy and the young women would stay the night, sleeping in the tent. 'They say they will start walking in the morning.'

'If they stop at Thinbottom I think I could get someone to give them and the cart a lift to Blandford.'

'You live at Thinbottom?'

'Me? I'm the vicar's daughter.'

'I'll give you a lift as soon as the ambulance has gone.'

'No need, thank you all the same,' she said, and, in case that had sounded rude, added, 'What I mean is, you've been awfully kind and it must have been a great nuisance to you. You'll be very late home. Besides, my bike's here.'

'The boy can load it on the cart and drop it off tomorrow when they get to Thinbottom. Won't your family be worried about you?'

'I went over to Frogwell Farm—Granny Coffin. Mother will think that I've stayed the night—she's very old and often ill.'

'Nevertheless, I must insist on seeing you to your home,' he said, and, when she would have protested, added, 'Please, don't argue—' He broke off. 'Ah, here's the ambulance at last.'

He went out of the tent to meet the paramedics, and when they reached the tent she slipped out and stood on one side while they undid their equipment and saw to his patient. Then, satisfied, he stood up and walked back to the ambulance with them, his patient and the baby and the father. As he passed the girl he said, 'Stay where you are,' in a voice that she couldn't ignore. In any case her bike was already roped onto the top of the hand-cart.

He came back presently. 'Shall we introduce ourselves?' he suggested. 'Gijs van Kessel.' He held out a large hand.

She shook it, feeling its firm grip. 'Margo Pearson,' she said, and then, 'That's not an English name—are you Dutch?'

'Yes. If you will wait a moment while I have a word with this boy...'

Once he had done so, he picked up his bag and, with the boy ahead of them with a torch, went back to the road and handed her into the car. Margo, sinking back against the leather softness, said, 'I've never been in a Rolls-Royce. It's very comfortable—and large too. But then you're a very large man, aren't you?' She sounded very matter-of-fact.

'Yes, I am. Miss Pearson, forgive me for mentioning it, but was it not rather foolhardy of you to rush into the road and stop a strange car? There are quite a few undesirable people around after dark.'

'I would have screamed very loudly if you had been one,' she told him sensibly. 'And I dare say Bert or Willy would have come.'

He didn't point out that by the time they could have reached her she might have been whisked away in the car or maltreated in some way.

They soon reached the village and she said, 'It's here on the left, by the church.'

He drew up at an open gateway. The house beyond was large and solid, a relic from the days when the parsonage had housed a cleric's large family, and overshadowed by the church a stone's throw from it. It, like the rest of the village, was in darkness, but as the doctor drew up a light shone through the transom over the front door.

'Thank you very much,' said Margo, and undid her seat belt.

He didn't reply, but got out of the car, opened her door and walked the few yards to the house with her. By the time they had reached the door it had been opened to reveal the vicar in his dressing gown.

'Margo—thank heaven. We had just phoned Frogwell Farm and been told that you left hours ago. You're all right? An accident?' He opened the door wide. 'Come in, both of you...'

'Father, this is Dr van Kessel, who kindly gave me a lift. There's been no accident but he has been of the greatest possible help.' She turned to greet her mother, a middle-aged replica of herself, as he and the vicar shook hands.

'My dear sir, we are in your debt. Come into the sitting room—a cup of coffee? Something to eat?'

'Thank you—but I'm on my way to Blandford to the hospital. Your daughter will explain. I am glad to have been of some help!' He smiled at Mrs Pearson. 'You have a very resourceful daughter, Mrs Pearson. I regret that I cannot stay and tell you of our evening's adventure, but I'm sure Miss Pearson will do so.'

He shook hands all round again, and Margo, having her hand gently crushed, had time to study him in the dim light of the hall. He had seemed enormous back there in the woods and he didn't seem any less so now. Not so very young, she decided. Mid-thirties, with fair hair already silvered, a commanding nose above a thin, firm mouth and startlingly blue eyes. She thought she would never forget him.

That he would forget her the moment he had resumed his journey went without saying; she had been a plain child and had grown into a plain young woman, and no one had ever pretended that she wasn't.

Her father had assured her that one could be beautiful as well as being possessed of mediocre features, and her mother thought of her lovingly as a *jolie laide*, but even George Merridew, who, in village parlance, was courting her cautiously, had told her with a well-meaning lack of tact that she might not have much in the way of good looks but she had plenty of common sense and was almost as good a cook as his mother.

A remark which Margo had found unsatisfactory. Surely if George was in love with her he should think of her as rather more than a cook and a sensible pair of hands? Or was that what he wanted? He was a good farmer and a prosperous man and she liked him—was even a little fond of him—but such remarks did nothing to endear him to her. And now this man had appeared from nowhere and gone again, and had left her feeling uncertain.

She related the night's happenings to her parents over a pot of tea and slices of bread and butter with lashings of jam. Caesar, the family cat, had curled up on her lap, and Plato, the elderly black Labrador, had got into his basket and gone back to sleep. She gobbled the last slice and sighed.

'I'm so sorry you were worried, but I couldn't leave them there, could I?'

'No, love, of course not. You did quite the right thing. They will bring your bicycle in the morning?'

'Oh, yes. I'm going to ask George to lend me the trailer, then they can put their hand-cart on it and go to Blandford.'

'Will George do that?' asked her father mildly.

'Well, he won't be using it until Wednesday, when he hauls the winter feed.'

Margo got up and tucked Caesar into Plato's basket. She put the mugs in the sink and said, 'It's after two o'clock. Don't either of you get up in the morning until I bring your tea. It's your morning off, isn't it, Father? I'll get the breakfast before I go to see George.'

It was still early when she drove over to George's farm in the worn out old Ford her father owned. His laconic, 'Hello, old girl,' was friendly enough, but hardly lover-like. He listened to her request without comment, only saying when she had finished, 'I don't see why not. I'm not needing it for a couple of days. But mind and drive carefully. Will you be at the whist drive this evening? Mother's going.'

Margo, who didn't like George's mother all that much, said that she'd see, and waited while he and one of his farmhands attached the trailer. She drove it care-fully back and then parked outside the vicarage in the main street, where the boy and the two young women would see it. She had just finished her breakfast when they came, pushing the hand-cart with her bike on top. They sat, the three of them, in the kitchen, drinking the tea her mother offered and eating bacon sandwiches, saying little.

The road was almost empty as she drove to Blandford Hospital, taking the by-roads she knew so well and getting there without mishap. She hadn't had any idea what was to happen next, but it seemed that the doctor had smoothed their path for them. There was an empty house near the hospital, they were told, and the travellers were to be allowed to stay in it until the mother and baby were fit to travel again.

The man who had come to speak to Margo at the

hospital looked at her curiously. He counted himself lucky to have been the casualty officer on duty when Professor van Kessel had arrived and sought his help last night. He was internationally well-known in his profession, and it had been a privilege to meet him. His fame as a paediatrician was widespread, and to have had the honour of meeting him... And he had been very accurate in his description of this Miss Pearson.

He said now, 'Mother and baby are doing well, but they'll have to stay for a couple of days. The professor found the empty house for her family. Don't ask me how at that time of night—the police, I suppose. I'll let you have the address. Oh, and he left some money for them. May I give it to you?'

'Professor?' asked Margo. 'Isn't he a doctor?'

The young doctor smiled down at her. She was rather sweet, even if plain, he thought.

'He's a famous man in the medical world. Specialises in children's illnesses.'

'Oh, I didn't know. I'll take the boy and the women to this house, shall I? They'll be all right there? I ought to get back in case the trailer is needed.'

'That's fine. The social services will have been told, and don't forget it's temporary—they can move on once the mother and baby are fit.'

It was a miserable little cottage, but it was empty and weatherproof. The boy unloaded the cart from the trailer, thanked her in a rather surly voice and, helped by the two young women, took their possessions indoors. Margo gave the money to one of the women. 'It's not from me. The doctor who looked after the baby left it for all of you,' she explained.

The woman gave her a sour look. 'We won't be staying here longer than we must.'

It was the other woman who called across, 'Well, thanks anyway.'

Margo drove back to George's farm and waited while the trailer was unhitched.

'Everything OK?' George wanted to know. 'Not done any damage?'

'No,' said Margo, and thought how delightful it would be if he would ask her—just once would do—if *she* was OK as well as the trailer. George, she felt sure, was a sound young man, steady and hardworking, but he hadn't much time for what he called all that nonsense. In due time he would marry, since a farmer needed a wife and sons to carry on his work, and she suspected that he had decided that she would do very nicely—little chance of her looks tempting any other suitors, a splendid cook, and capable of turning her hand to anything.

Margo drove the short distance back to the vicarage, childishly wishing for a miracle—glossy fair curls, blue eyes and a face to make men turn to look at her twice and then fall in love with her. 'And not just George,' she said aloud. 'Someone like Dr van Kessel—no, Professor van Kessel. Someone handsome, rich and important. He won't even remember what I look like.'

He remembered—though perhaps not quite as she would have wished. His patient comfortably settled and the help of the police sought, after a friendly chat with the young doctor on call in Casualty he had been free to drive himself back to London.

He'd taken the Salisbury road, and then the rather lonely road through Stockridge until he'd reached the M3. There had been little traffic—even the city streets, when he'd reached them, had been tolerably quiet.

When he was in England he stayed with an old friend

and colleague, and since his work took him to various big teaching hospitals he came and went freely, using his borrowed key. He'd stopped silently in a mews behind a terrace of townhouses, garaged his car and walked round to the street, let himself in and had gone silently to his room for the few hours of sleep left to him.

He hadn't been tired; lack of sleep didn't bother him unduly; it was a hazard of his profession. He had lain for a while, remembering with amusement the girl who had brought him to such a sudden halt. A small girl, totally without fear and sensible. Bossy too! He had no doubt at all that she would see her protégés safely housed. He wondered idly how she would get them to Blandford. He had no doubt that she would...

The professor had a busy week. Outpatients' clinics where he had to deal with anxious mothers as well as sick children, small patients for whom his specialised surgery had been required to be visited in the wards and a theatre list which, however hard he worked, never seemed to grow smaller.

An urgent call came from Birmingham during the week, asking him to operate on a child with one leg inches shorter than its fellow. It was something in which he specialised, the straightening and correction of malformed bones in children and babies, and he was much in demand. Totally absorbed, he forgot Margo.

Margo was busy too, although her tasks were of a more mundane nature—flowers for the church, the last of the apples and pears to pick from the old trees behind the vicarage, getting the church hall ready for the monthly whist drive, cutting sandwiches for the Mothers' Union annual party, driving her mother into Sturminster

Newton for the weekly shopping… Unlike Professor van Kessel, however, she hadn't forgotten.

Waiting patiently in the village shop while Mrs Drew, the village gossip, chose the cheese she liked and at the same time passed on an embroidered version of the rumpus at Downend Farm when the bull had broken loose, Margo allowed her thoughts to dwell on the man who had come into her life so abruptly and gone again without trace. She was still thinking about him as she left the shop, clutching the breakfast bacon, when she was hailed from a passing motor car.

It stopped within a few feet of her and the elderly driver called her over.

'Margo—the very person I am on my way to see. Get in. We will go back to the house, where we can talk.' He noticed her shopping basket. 'Want to go home first?'

'Well, yes, please, Sir William. Mother expects me back. Can't we talk at home?'

'Yes, yes, of course…'

'I'll not get in, then. You can park in the drive; the gate's open.'

She crossed the narrow street and was waiting for him as he stopped by the door. Sir William Frost greeted Mrs Pearson with pleasant friendliness, accepted the offer of coffee and followed Margo into the sitting room.

'Want to ask a favour of you, Margo. You saw Imogen in church, didn't you?' he asked, referring to his granddaughter. 'Been staying with us for a few days. Intended to take her up to town myself, but got this directors' meeting in Exeter. Can't spare Tomkins; want him to stay at the house with Lady Frost. Wondered if you'd drive her up to her aunt's place in town. Don't care to send her by train.'

Mrs Pearson came in with the coffee and Sir William repeated himself all over again, then sat back and drank his coffee. He was a short, stout man, with a drooping moustache and a weatherbeaten face, liked by everyone despite the fact that he liked his own way with everything. And, even if from time to time he rode roughshod over someone's feelings, his wife, a small, dainty little lady, quickly soothed them over.

He finished his coffee, accepted a second cup and said, 'Well?'

Margo said in her sensible way, 'Yes, of course I'll take her, Sir William. When do you want her to go?'

'Day after tomorrow. Get there in time for lunch. Much obliged to you, Margo.'

It was the vicar who unknowingly upset the plans. His car wouldn't be available—he had been bidden to see his bishop on the very day Imogen was to be driven to her aunt's house.

Sir William huffed and puffed when he was informed. 'Then you will have to go by train. I'll get the local taxi to take you to Sherborne. Get another taxi at Paddington. Not what I wanted, but it can't be helped, I suppose.'

Imogen, fifteen years old, wilful, spoilt and convinced that she was quite grown-up, was delighted. Life, she confided to Margo, was boring. For most of the year she was at boarding-school while her father—something in the diplomatic service—and mother lived in an obscure and unsettled part of Europe, which meant that she was ferried to and fro between members of the family in England.

She made no secret of her boredom while staying
with her grandparents—but the aunt in London offered
the delights of theatres and shopping. Imogen, recov-
ering from a severe attack of measles, intended to enjoy
her sick leave before going back to school.

Of course, she disliked the idea of being taken to her
aunt's as though she were a child, but she got on quite
well with Margo and it was nice to have someone to
see to the boring things like tickets and taxis.

They made the journey together more or less in harmony, although Margo had to discourage her from using a particularly vivid lipstick and eyeliner the moment the taxi was out of her grandfather's gates.

'Why not wait until you are in London?' suggested
Margo, being tactful. 'You will be able to consult one
of those young ladies behind a cosmetic counter and
get the very best and the latest.'

Imogen reluctantly agreed. 'You could do with some
decent make-up yourself,' she observed with youthful
candour. 'But I suppose that as you're the vicar's
daughter it doesn't matter how you look.'

Margo, trying to think of the right answer to this,
gave up and said nothing.

It was quite a lengthy ride from Paddington to
Imogen's aunt's house—a substantial town residence in
a terrace of well-maintained homes.

Strictly for the wealthy, reflected Margo, getting out
of the taxi to pay the cabby. It would be interesting to
see inside…

They were admitted by a blank-faced butler who informed them that they were expected and showed them
into a small room furnished with little gilt chairs which
looked as though they would collapse if anyone sat on
them, a hideous marble-topped table and an arrangement of flowers on a tall stand.

'Lady Mellor will be with you presently,' they were told, and were left to perch uneasily on the chairs. But only for a few minutes. Suddenly the door was thrust open and Lady Mellor made a brisk entry.

'Dearest child,' she exclaimed in a penetrating voice, and embraced her niece before adding, 'And your companion. Your grandfather said that you would have suitable company for your journey.'

She smiled briefly at Margo, then turned to Imogen and said, 'Your little cousin is rather poorly. The specialist is with him at the moment, but as soon as he has gone we will have lunch together and a good chat.' She turned back to Margo. 'If you'd care to wait in the hall I'll arrange for some refreshment for you before you return home. I'm sure I am much obliged to you for taking care of Imogen.'

Margo murmured politely that refreshment would be welcome, as breakfast had been at a very early hour. She sat down in the chair indicated by Lady Mellor and watched her walk away with Imogen. She had been thanked and forgotten.

Her stomach rumbled and she hoped for a sandwich at least.

She had been sitting there for five minutes or more when she heard the murmur of voices, and two men, deep in talk, came down the staircase slowly. One was an elderly man who looked tired, and with him was Professor van Kessel. They stood in the hall, murmuring together, with the butler hovering in the background, ready to show them out.

They were on the point of leaving the house when Professor van Kessel, glancing around him, saw Margo. He bade his colleague goodbye and crossed the hall to her.

'Miss Pearson. So we meet again—although rather unexpectedly.'

She didn't try to hide her delight at seeing him again. 'I brought Imogen—Sir William's granddaughter—up to London to stay with her aunt. I'm going back again very shortly, but I'm to have some kind of meal first. I was told to wait here.'

'I have an appointment now, but I shall be free in an hour,' said the professor. 'Wait here; I'll drive you back. I'm going that way,' he added vaguely.

'Well, thank you, but won't they mind? I mean, can I just sit here until you come?'

'I don't see why not. I shall be here again probably before you have had your lunch.' He smiled down at her. 'Whatever you do, don't go away.'

'No, all right, I won't. If you're sure…'

'Quite sure,' he told her placidly. 'I'll see you within the hour.'

She watched him go, and the butler closed the door behind him and went away.

It was all right at first. It was quiet and pleasantly warm and her chair was comfortable; the minutes ticked away and she thought longingly of coffee and sandwiches. At any moment, she told herself, someone would come and lead her to wherever she was to have the refreshments offered to her.

No one came. Fifteen minutes, half an hour went past, and although from time to time she heard a door open or close no one came into the hall. If she hadn't promised Professor van Kessel that she would wait for him she would have left the house. Margo, used to the willing hospitality of the vicarage, felt in an alien world. The magnificent long-case clock across the hall struck half past one, almost drowning the sound of the doorbell, and as though waiting for his cue the butler went to answer it.

Professor van Kessel came into the hall unhurriedly. 'I've not kept you waiting?' he wanted to know cheerfully. 'You've finished your lunch?'

Margo stood up, her insides rumbling again. 'I haven't had lunch,' she said with asperity. 'I have been sitting here…' She gave the butler a nasty look.

His poker face became almost human. 'I am indeed sorry, Miss. We had no orders concerning you. I had assumed that you had left the house.' He gave the doctor a nervous glance. 'If the professor would wait, I can bring coffee and sandwiches…'

Margo, her thoughts diverted from her insides, gave the doctor a thoughtful look. 'Should I call you Professor?'

'It's only another name for Doctor.' He turned to the butler. 'I'll give Miss Pearson lunch. I'm sure it was no fault of yours. Explain to your mistress, will you?'

He whisked Margo out of the house then and into his car. As he drove away he asked, 'When are you expected home?'

'I was going to get the three-thirty from Paddington.'

'Oh, good. We shall have time for a leisurely meal before we start for home.'

She said awkwardly, 'Just coffee and sandwiches would do. It's just that I had breakfast rather early.'

'So did I. And I haven't had time for lunch.' He uttered the fib in a placid voice which reassured her.

'Oh, well—I dare say you're hungry.'

'Indeed I am.' He resolutely forgot the lamb cutlets followed by the substantial apple tart that he had been offered at the hospital. 'I know a very pleasant little restaurant five minutes from here.'

'I expect you know Lady Mellor?' asked Margo, making conversation.

'Never heard of her before this morning. Her doctor asked me for a second opinion on her small son. A pampered brat who needed his bottom smacked. He got at the wine decanter and was first drunk and then sick. No one had thought to ask him what he'd had to eat or drink.' He slowed the car. 'A waste of my time. There's a meter—we're in luck.'

The restaurant was close by and only half-full. Margo gave him an eloquent glance and sped away to the Ladies', and when she got back found him at a table by the window, studying the menu. He got up as she reached him, took her jacket and handed it to the waiter, then said, 'You deserve a drink. Would you like sherry?'

'You can't have one—you're driving—so I won't either. I'd like tonic and lemon, please.'

He waited as she took a menu from the waiter. 'We have plenty of time; choose whatever you would like.'

The menu was mouthwatering and, since there were no prices, probably very expensive. Margo decided on an omelette and salad, thereby endearing herself to the doctor, who chose the same, thankful that when she chose sticky toffee pudding with cream to follow he could settle for biscuits and cheese.

Presently, as she poured their coffee, he was pleased to see that she had a pretty colour in her cheeks now, and a well-fed look. Shabby treatment, he reflected, to leave her sitting there without so much as a glass of water...

He asked idly, 'Do you often run errands for anyone who asks?'

'Well, yes. You see, Father always helps anyone who

needs it, and of course that means Mother and I help
out too.'

'You would not wish for a different life?'

'I haven't any training, have I?' she reminded him.
'I'd love to travel...' Just for a moment she looked
wistful. 'But life isn't dull. There's always something
happening, even in a small village like Thinbottom.'

'You don't hanker for life in London?'

'Goodness me, no. Do you like living here,
Professor?'

'Don't, I beg you, call me Professor; it makes me
feel elderly. No, I don't like living here—my home is
in Holland. I only come here from time to time. I stay
with an old friend and, though I'm too busy to go out
much, I do have other friends scattered around the
country with whom I spend my weekends when I'm
free.'

'You're going back to Holland soon?'

Her heart sank when he said, 'Oh, yes, in a few
weeks—I have to be back there for Christmas.'

Soon after, they got back into the car, and, encouraged by his questions, she gave him an account of the
travellers.

'I went to see them in that house you found for them.
The baby's a darling. They plan to move on but they'll
be all right; they were given clothes and blankets and
they didn't seem to mind that they hadn't a van. I wish
I knew someone...'

'They'll probably strike lucky. The weather is good,
and that should be a great help to them.' He glanced at
his watch. 'Shall we stop for tea, or would you like to
get home as quickly as possible?'

'Well, by the time we're home it will be teatime. If
you can spare the time I know Mother would love to

give you a cup. You don't need to stay if you're going further.'

He hid a smile. 'That does sound delightful.' He began to talk about the country they were passing through, careful to put her at her ease.

CHAPTER TWO

THEY reached the vicarage shortly before five o'clock, and Margo led the way in through the open front door to be met by her mother's voice.

'Is that you, love? You're early...' Mrs Pearson's head appeared round the kitchen door. 'Dr van Kessel, how nice to see you. You'll stay for tea? It's in the dining room—I thought that Margo might be hungry...'

'You'll stay?' asked Margo. 'That is, if you'd like to.'

'Indeed I would. Thank you, Mrs Pearson—if you don't mind having an uninvited guest. I happened to meet Margo, and it seemed sensible to give her a lift as I was driving this way myself.'

'Now that was kind of you. Take off your coat, and you too, Margo, and go and fetch your father. You come with me, Doctor...'

'He's a professor, Mother,' said Margo quickly.

'He's Gijs to his friends.' He glanced at Margo and smiled. 'And I hope Margo will allow me to call her Margo...'

'Of course you may, if you want to. Everyone does.'

She gave him a wide smile and skimmed away to fetch her father from his study.

Sitting beside his hostess presently, Gijs reflected that it was a very long time since he had sat down to a substantial tea. At the hospital he drank the cups of tea brought to him and often drank them tepid, since he hadn't the time to stop in his work. If he wasn't at the hospital but at his consulting rooms, his secretary would sneak him a cup between patients—but five o'clock tea, such as this was, was a rarity. Sliced bread and butter arranged on a pretty plate, jam, honey, a covered dish of buttered toast, scones and a large fruit cake. Moreover, the tea was hot and strong, with plenty of milk.

'I don't suppose you have much time for tea,' observed Mrs Pearson chattily. 'Last time I was in London with the Women's Institute we had tea at a hotel—little teapots barely enough for one cup and quite nasty looks from the waitresses when we asked for more hot water. And such mean little sandwiches and cakes. I dare say that's fashionable. Where did you see Margo?'

'At Lady Mellor's house. I'm sure that Margo can tell you about it better than I.'

Margo told. 'I dare say Lady Mellor had a lot to worry about,' she finished, 'and the butler was very nice about it. It wasn't anyone's fault, if you see what I mean.'

From anyone else, thought the professor, that would sound priggish, but somehow not from Margo—she is, after all, the vicar's daughter, brought up to see good in everyone. Let's hope she'll never be disillusioned.

He said lightly then, 'It was just our good luck that we should meet in such an unlikely place. I'm delighted to have had company driving down here.'

'You like England?' asked the vicar.

'Very much.' The two men started a discussion about the English countryside, but the professor volunteered no real information about his own country. Certainly he enlarged upon the social and commercial aspects, and enlarged too upon his homeland, albeit rather vaguely, but Margo reflected that he had told them nothing of his own home or where he lived. Perhaps he was married...

The thought was an unwelcome one which she thrust aside. Why shouldn't he be married with a brood of children? It was none of her business. She did want to know, however.

Margo being Margo, it was no sooner said than done.

'Are you married?' she asked him. Then regretted it the moment she had spoken; the look of amused surprise on his face sent the colour into her cheeks and she mumbled, 'Sorry, that was rude of me...'

'No, I'm not married.' He ignored the mumble. 'I have never found the time.'

Mrs Pearson hastened to fill an awkward pause. 'Of course one always expects doctors to be family men— I'm sure I don't know why. A wife and children must be a hindrance to their work at times.'

He smiled. 'I imagine that doctors' wives quickly learn not to be that—rather, a pleasant distraction after a long day's work. And my married colleagues are doting fathers.'

'Then you should make haste and marry,' observed Mrs Pearson.

The vicar put his dignified oar in. 'I'm sure that Gijs will marry when he wishes to do so, my dear.' He added thoughtfully, 'I wonder why a patient should expect his or her doctor to be a married man? It's an interesting point.'

So started an interesting discussion in which Margo took no part. She passed the cake, handed cups of tea round and wished herself elsewhere. Which was silly— after all, she hadn't been very rude. She should have laughed it off for the trivial remark it had been, instead of feeling as though she had been nosey. Perhaps, horror of horrors, now he would think that she was intent on attracting him. He wouldn't want any more to do with her. He would go away and she would never see him again. If she had been witty and pretty and charming, it might have been a different matter...

Professor van Kessel was either a man with the kindest heart imaginable or was prone to deafness; he apparently hadn't heard her muttered apology. The conversation flowed smoothly, and presently, when he got up to go, he bade her goodbye with his usual pleasant detachment. He didn't say he hoped to see her again, however.

Watching the Rolls-Royce gliding away towards the village, Margo told herself that he'd gone for good and she could forget him. Whether she wanted to forget him was an entirely different matter, and one she was reluctant to consider.

To her mother's observation that it was a pity that they were unlikely to see him again, she replied airily that it had been pleasant meeting him once more and that she supposed he would be returning to Holland. 'After all, it is his home,' she said.

She collected the tea things and carried them out to the kitchen. 'I thought I'd go over to see Mrs Merridew tomorrow afternoon. George said she might like some help with the jam. They've a huge plum harvest this year.'

Her mother gave her a thoughtful look. Despite the fact that George's mother had made no secret of the fact that she considered Margo to be a suitable wife for him, the woman had no affection for her. She was, thought Mrs Pearson shrewdly, under the impression that once Margo married she would be able to mould her into the kind of wife she felt her George should have. That Margo wasn't a girl to be moulded had never entered her head. She had too good an opinion of herself to realise that Margo didn't like her over-

much, but bore with her overbearing ways for George's
sake.

Mrs Pearson, knowing in her bones that Margo didn't
love George, told herself to have patience. Somewhere
in the world there was a man for her Margo—preferably
the counterpart of Gijs van Kessel...

So Margo took herself off the next day to Merridew's
Farm, intent on being nice to everyone, doing her best
to keep her thoughts on a future when she would marry
George and live there, and failing lamentably because
she thought about the professor instead.

However, once she was at the farm, he was banished
from her head by Mrs Merridew's loud, hectoring voice
bidding her to join her in the kitchen.

'I can do with some help,' she greeted Margo.
'There's an apron behind the door; you can stone the
plums... You should have worn a sensible sweater; if
you get stains on that blouse they'll never come out.'

I have never known anybody, reflected Margo, rolling up her sleeves, who could put a damper on any
occasion, however trivial. She began to stone the
plums—a messy business—and paused in her work as
the thought that she couldn't possibly marry George
suddenly entered her head.

'Why have you stopped?' Mrs Merridew wanted to
know. 'There's another bucketful in the pantry. I'm
sure I don't know why I should have to do everything
myself; you'll have to change your ways when you
marry George.'

Margo said nothing—there was no point at the moment. Besides, she was busy composing a suitable
speech for George's benefit.

He wouldn't mind, she reflected. He was fond of her,
just as she was fond of him, but being fond wasn't the

same as being in love. She wasn't sure why she was so certain about that. A future with George had loomed before her for several years now—everyone had taken it for granted that when the time came they would marry, and she had got used to the idea and accepted it; she wanted to marry, she wanted children and a husband to care for her, and at twenty-eight she was sure that romance—the kind of romance she read about in novels—had passed her by.

But romance had touched her with feather-light fingers in the shape of Gijs van Kessel, and life would never be the same again.

She glanced across the table at Mrs Merridew, who was a formidable woman, tall and stout, with her iron-grey hair permanently waved into rock-like formations and a mouth which seldom smiled. She was respected in the village but not liked as her long-dead husband had been liked, and she was always ready to find fault. Only with George was she softer in her manner...

'Fetch me the other preserving pan, Margo.' Mrs Merridew's voice cut into her thoughts. 'I'll get this first batch on the stove. By the time you've finished stoning that lot I can fill a second pan.'

Margo went to the far wall and got down the copper preserving pan and put it on the table.

'Cat got your tongue?' asked Mrs Merridew. 'Never known you so quiet. What's all this nonsense I heard about you and a pack of tramps?'

'Not tramps—travellers. And it wasn't nonsense. One of them had a baby by the side of the road.'

'More fool her,' declared Mrs Merridew. 'These people bring shame to the countryside.'

'Why?' asked Margo, and ate a plum.

'Why? They're dirty and dishonest and live from hand to mouth.'

'Well, they looked clean enough to me,' said Margo. 'And I don't know that they're dishonest—no more so than people who live in houses...'

Her companion snorted. 'Rubbish! If any of them came onto the farm George would soon send them packing.'

'Would he? Would he really? Or would he do it to please you?'

Mrs Merridew went red. 'You don't seem yourself today, Margo. I hope you're not ill—picked up something nasty from those tramps.'

She set the pan of fruit on the old-fashioned stove. 'While that's coming to the boil we'll have a cup of tea, then you'd better go home. I dare say you've a cold coming.'

Margo never wanted to see another plum; she agreed meekly, drank her tea, washed the cups and saucers in the sink, bade Mrs Merridew goodbye and got on her bike. She had wanted to talk to George but she wasn't to be given the chance. She would come up early in the morning; he would be in the cow parlour and there would be time to talk.

'Early back, dear,' commented her mother as she came in through the kitchen door. 'Weren't you asked to stay for tea?'

Margo sat down at the table and watched her mother rolling dough for scones. 'No. Mrs Merridew thinks I may have caught a cold.' Margo popped a piece of dough into her mouth. 'Mother, I don't want to marry George...'

Mrs Pearson was cutting rounds of dough and arranging them on a baking tray. 'Your father and I have always hoped that you wouldn't, although we would never have said anything if you had. You don't love him.'

'No. I like him—I'm fond of him—but that's not the same, is it?'

'No, love, it isn't. When you do fall in love you'll know that. Have you told George?'

'I'll go and see him tomorrow early. Do you think he'll be upset?'

Her mother put the scones in the oven. 'No, dear, I don't. George is a nice young man but I think he wants a wife, not a woman to love. She'll need to be fond of him, of course, and he of her, but that will be sufficient. And that wouldn't be sufficient for you, would it?'

'No. I would like,' said Margo thoughtfully, 'to be cosseted and spoilt and loved very much, and I'd want to be allowed to be me, if you see what I mean. I would be a good wife and have lots of children because we would have enough money to keep us all in comfort.' She laughed a little. 'Aren't I silly? But I'm sure about George, Mother. I'd rather stay single…'

'I know you are doing the right thing, love. See what your father says.'

Margo laid the table for tea and presently, over that meal, the Reverend Mr Pearson voiced his opinion that Margo was indeed doing the right thing. 'And if you feel unsettled for a while, my dear, why not go and stay with one of your aunts? Heaven knows, your mother and I have enough relations to choose from.'

'I'd be running away…'

'No, clearing the decks. And you wouldn't go for a week or two. Give the village a chance to discuss it thoroughly.' They all laughed. 'There's not much happening until the bazaar; it'll liven things up a bit.'

Margo was up early, dressed and on her bike while it still wasn't quite light, and was in plenty of time to see George while the cows were being milked.

She leaned her bike against a pile of logs and, her heart thumping hard despite her resolution to keep calm, went into the cow parlour.

Two of the cowmen were already milking, and George was standing by the door checking some equipment. He looked up when she went in.

'Good Lord, what brings you here at this time of the morning? Mother said you were sickening for a cold. Don't come near me, whatever you do.'

Not a very encouraging beginning, but Margo braced herself.

'I haven't got a cold. Your mother just thought I might have one because I didn't talk much...!'

'Won't do not to get on with Mother,' said George. A rebuke she ignored.

'I wanted to talk to you for a minute or two—this is the only time when we're alone.'

'Well, let's have it, old girl. I've not got all day.'

It was being called 'old girl' which started her off. 'You have never asked me, George, but everyone seems to think that we will marry. Perhaps you don't intend to ask me, but if you do don't bother, because I don't want to marry you. I would make a very bad farmer's wife—and your mother would live with us.'

'Well, of course she would—show you how things are done before she takes her ease and you take over.'

The prospect left Margo short of breath. She persevered, though. 'George, do you love me?'

'What's got into you, girl? We've known each other almost all our lives.'

'Yes, I know that. That's not what I meant. Are you in love with me? Do I excite you? Do you want to give me the moon and the stars?'

'You're crazy, Margo. What's that twaddle got to do with being a good wife?'

'I'm not sure, but I think it must have a great deal to do with it. So you won't mind very much if we don't get married? You're a very nice person, George. There must be dozens of girls who'd give anything to be your wife.'

'Well, as to that, I reckon that's so. Mother always had her doubts, even though she liked the idea of me marrying the vicar's daughter.'

Margo swallowed her rage. 'Well, that leaves everyone quite satisfied, doesn't it?' She turned to go. 'Pass the news around the village, will you? I'm glad your heart isn't broken!'

She got onto her bike and pedalled home as though the Furies were after her. She knew that George hadn't meant to be unkind, but she felt as though he really didn't mind one way or the other—and that was very lowering to a girl who hadn't had much of an opinion of herself in the first place.

To her mother's carefully worded question she gave a matter-of-fact account of her meeting with George. 'So that's that,' she finished briskly. 'And if you don't mind I *would* quite like to go away for a week or two.'

'You need a change,' declared her mother. 'There's so little life here for someone young. I know you're kept busy, but a change of scene... Have you any idea where you'd like to go?'

The vicar looked up from his cornflakes. 'Your aunt Florence, when she last wrote, expressed the view that she would be glad to see any of us who cared to visit her. Sunningfield is a village even smaller than this one, but it is near Windsor and within easy reach of London and I believe she has many friends. Your uncle was a very respected and popular man during his lifetime.'

He passed his cup for more coffee. 'I will telephone

her this morning and drive you there myself if you would like that?'

Truth to tell, Margo didn't much mind where she went. All she knew was that she would like to get away for a little while and think. She wasn't sure what it was she needed to think about, but think she must. She wasn't upset about calling off the vague future George had sketched out for her from time to time, but she felt restless and she didn't know why. A week or two with Aunt Flo would put everything back into its right perspective once more.

It was arranged that she should go in four or five days' time, and in the meantime that gave the village the opportunity to adjust to the idea that she and George weren't to be married after all. She would have been surprised at the number of people who expressed their satisfaction at that.

'There'd have been no life for Miss Margo with that Mrs Merridew,' observed the verger's wife. 'Nice little lady, that Miss Margo is. Good luck to her, I says!' A sentiment which was shared by many.

Margo countered the questions from the well-meaning among her father's congregation in her sensible way, packed a bag with the best of her wardrobe and was presently driven to Sunningfield.

Aunt Florence lived at the end of the village in a cottage which had at one time been the gamekeeper's home on the local estate. Lord Trueman, having fallen on bad times, had prudently let or sold the lodges and estate cottages, being careful to see that the occupants were suitable neighbours. And of course Aunt Florence was eminently suitable. What could be more respectable than an archdeacon's widow?

They arrived in time for tea and, admitted by a beaming young girl, were led across the hall where she threw open a door and said cheerfully, 'Here they are, ma'am. I'll fetch the tea.'

Aunt Flo rose to meet them. A tall, bony lady with short curly hair going white, she had a sharp nose and a sharp tongue too, both of which concealed a warm heart. She embraced them briskly, told them to make themselves comfortable, and when the girl brought in the teatray offered refreshment. At the same time she gave and received family news.

It was when this topic had been exhausted that she asked, 'And you, Margo? You have decided not to marry that young farmer? I must say I never thought much of the idea. You are entirely unsuited to the life of a farmer's wife; I cannot imagine how you came to consider it in the first place.'

'No one had ever asked me to marry them, Aunt Flo. Well, George didn't exactly ask; we just kind of drifted, if you see what I mean. We've known each other for years...'

'That's no reason to marry. One marries for love— or should do. You're not so old that you need despair, although I must say it is a pity that you haven't the Pearson good looks.'

A remark which Margo took in good part, seeing that it was true. They had supper after her father had driven away, and Aunt Florence outlined the various treats she had in store for her niece.

'You have brought a pretty dress with you? Good. We are invited to Lord Trueman's place for drinks after church. You will meet most of my friends and acquaintances there—a good start.'

Aunt Florence lived in some style, even if in somewhat reduced circumstances. Her little house was well furnished and Margo's bedroom was pretty as well as comfortable. Life for Aunt Flo was placid and pleasant. The cheerful girl—Phoebe—came each day and cleaned, and did most of the cooking before she left in the evening, and an old man from the village saw to the heavy work in the garden—although Aunt Flo did the planting and planning. Even at the tail-end of the year, it was a charming little spot, surrounded by shrubs and small trees, tidied up ready for the winter.

Margo felt quite at home within twenty-four hours— joining her aunt in her daily walk and playing cards in the evening, or watching whichever programme her aunt thought suitable, with Moses, the ginger Persian cat, on her knee. On the next Sunday she accompanied her aunt to church and afterwards walked up the drive to the rather ugly early Victorian house built by Lord Trueman's ancestor on the site of the charming Elizabethan mansion he had disliked.

'Hideous,' observed Aunt Florence, and added, 'It's simply frightful inside.'

There were a lot of people gathered in an immense room with panelled walls and a great deal of heavy furniture. Margo was taken to one group after another by Lady Trueman, a middle-aged lady with a sweet face, and introduced to a great many people whose names she instantly forgot.

'Now do come and meet my daughter,' said Lady Trueman. 'She's staying with us for a week or two. I've a small granddaughter too—Peggy. She's a handful— three years old.' She had fetched up in front of a young woman not much older than Margo herself.

'Helen, this is Margo Pearson—come to stay with Mrs Pearson. I've been telling her about Peggy...'

She trotted away and left them to talk. Helen was nice, Margo decided. They talked about clothes and toddlers and babies, and presently slipped upstairs to the nursery to see Peggy, an imp of mischief if ever there was one, who took no notice of her nurse—a young girl, kind enough, no doubt, but lacking authority.

'Such a naughty puss,' said her mother lovingly. 'We never know what she will do next.'

Back in Aunt Flo's house over lunch, that lady expressed the opinion that the child was being spoilt. 'A dear child, but that nurse of hers is no good—far too easygoing.'

The days went by with a pleasant monotony: shopping in the village, visiting her aunt's friends for coffee or tea. And if Margo sometimes wished for a little excitement she squashed the thought at once. Her aunt was kindness itself, and she was sure that the holiday was doing her a lot of good. Taking her mind off things. Well, George for instance. The unbidden thought that she wished that it would take her mind off Professor van Kessel too was another thought to be squashed.

She thought about him far too often, although she tried not to. It wasn't so difficult when she was with her aunt, whose conversation was of a sort to require close attention and sensible answers at intervals, but when she was on her own, doing an errand for her or in the garden, grubbing up the few weeds which had hoped to escape that lady's eye, there was ample time for reflection.

So silly, Margo told herself one day, on her way back from taking a pot of Mrs Pearson's jam to an acquaintance who had expressed a wish to try it. It had been quite a long walk and the afternoon was already sliding briskly into dusk. What was more, it was going to rain at any moment. Margo, taking a short cut across Lord

Trueman's park, abandoned her pleasant daydreaming and put her best foot forward.

The park was vast, and this far from the house, which was just visible in the distance, its planned trees and shrubs had given way to rough ground, a ploughed field or two and sparse woodland through which ran a small stream, swollen now by October rains. The right of way ran beside it for some way and then turned away to join a wider path, leading back to one of the lodges some half a mile away.

Margo walked fast, head down against the rain, which was coming down in earnest now, thankful that she would soon join the path. It was pure chance that she gave a quick glance around her as she stopped to turn up the collar of her jacket. It was a movement in the stream some yards away which had caught her eye—a small, scarlet-clad figure, half in, half out of the water, a small arm trailing gently to and fro, washed by the stream as it raced along.

Margo ran through the rough grass and waded across the water, slipping and sliding, losing a shoe and not noticing, bent on getting to the child as quickly as possible.

It was Peggy, her head, thank heaven, on the bank, but most of her small person in the water. She was unconscious and Margo soon saw why: there was a big bruise on her forehead. She had fallen awkwardly and Margo had a few anxious moments hauling her out of the stream and up the bank. This done, there was the necessity to cross the stream again, for behind her was nothing but wooded country going nowhere.

It's amazing what you can do when you have to, reflected Margo, slipping and sliding across to the other bank with Peggy hoisted awkwardly over a shoulder. Once there, there was the urgent need to get to the house, for as far as she could see there was no other help nearby.

Hoisting the little girl more securely, Margo started off across the field to where, in the distance, she could see the lights of the house.

It was raining in earnest now, hard cold rain which soaked them even more than they already were. Margo squelched along in her one shoe and thought that she would never reach the outer edge of the landscaped park around the house. She paused for a moment to hitch Peggy onto her other shoulder and trudged on. Surely by now they would have missed the child and there would be a search party? It would be a waste of precious breath to shout, she decided, worried now that perhaps she should have tried to revive the child before setting out for the house. Supposing the moppet died? She had felt a faint pulse when she had reached Peggy, but she hadn't tried to do anything else.

She was near the house now, close to its grand entrance. She climbed the broad steps and gave the iron bell-pull by the door a terrific tug. Just to make sure, she tugged again. And again…

The door opened slowly under the indignant hand of Bush, the butler, who was affronted by the misuse of the bell-pull and the excessive noise. He had his mouth open to voice his displeasure, but Margo gave him no chance to utter a word.

'Get a doctor quickly, and get Lady Trueman or her daughter—anyone. Only hurry!'

She pushed past him and made for the stairs, dripping across the hall, short of breath, waterlogged and terrified. There was no time to give way to terror. She drew a breath.

'Will someone come quickly? I've got Peggy…'

She saw the butler hurry to the phone as a door

opened and Lady Trueman, followed by her daughter, came into the hall.

'What is all this noise…?' She goggled at Margo. 'Peggy—she's ill? What has happened? It's Margo Pearson…'

Margo didn't waste time explaining. 'Get her clothes off. She's been in the stream; she's unconscious. She must be rubbed dry and put to bed. I told the butler to get a doctor. Only will someone please hurry…?'

'My baby!' wailed Helen. 'Where's the nurse…?'

We shall be here all day, thought Margo, asking silly questions. She started up the stairs, intent on getting to the nursery, calling over her shoulder, 'Is the doctor coming? It's urgent. And for heaven's sake will someone give me a hand?'

This time her appeal was heard. The housekeeper, made aware of the commotion, had come into the hall and now hurried up the staircase to Margo.

'The nursery's on the next floor. Can you manage? I'll go ahead and turn down the bedclothes and get the place warmed.'

By the time Margo had reached the nursery she was standing ready with towels, the fire poked up and the lights on.

'Let me have her on my lap. Get your wet things off, miss. You'll catch your death. In the stream? You found her and carried her here? Bless you for that, miss. Where's that nurse of hers, I'd like to know—?'

She broke off to speak to Lady Trueman, who had just tottered in.

'Now, my lady, keep calm. Peggy will be all right, thanks to this brave young lady. Get your maid to give you a glass of brandy and give one to Miss Helen— and send Bessy up here, please.'

Helen had joined her mother. 'Peggy—out in all that rain—where's the nurse?'

The housekeeper said briskly, 'That's the doorbell, Miss Helen. Go and fetch the doctor up, will you? No time to waste.'

Margo, dragging off her wet shoe, her jacket a sodden heap on the floor, reflected that this housekeeper and her aunt Flo would make a splendid pair in any emergency.

Bessy came, and then was sent away to fetch a glass of brandy for Margo.

'I never drink it,' said Margo.

'Just this once you will, miss.' The housekeeper was firm. 'It's either that or pneumonia.'

So Margo tossed back the brandy, caught her breath at its fiery strength and felt a pleasant warmth from it. Perhaps she could take off the rest of her clothes... No, not yet. The doctor, ushered in by a weeping Helen, was bending over Peggy, who was now wrapped in a warm blanket on the housekeeper's lap.

She was still unconscious, and there was a large bump under the bruise.

'Will someone tell me what has happened?' The doctor was youngish and cheerful. 'It would help if just one of you could tell me.'

'Ask the young lady here,' said the housekeeper, and waved towards the shivering Margo. 'She found her and carried her here. A proper heroine.'

Margo, a trifle muzzy with the brandy, nonetheless managed a sensible account of what had happened, and then lapsed into silence.

'You undoubtedly saved Peggy's life,' said the doctor. 'She's concussed, but she's warm and her pulse is good. She must be X-rayed, of course, but not for the moment. Just bed and warmth and someone to be with her in case she comes round. How come she was so far from home?'

'I don't know where her nurse has got to. She should have been in the nursery, or playing in the garden with her. I—we—Mother and I were in the drawing room...' said Helen feebly.

'I want a second opinion,' said Lady Trueman. 'Will you get the very best consultant to come as soon as possible?'

The doctor got up. 'Yes, certainly, Lady Trueman. If I might use your phone, I know just the man.' He paused at the doorway. 'I think it might be a good idea if someone were to see to this young lady. A warm bath and a hot drink, and get those wet clothes off—a warm blanket or something.' He looked grim. 'But for her, you might have lost Peggy.'

He went over to Margo and picked up her wrist. 'Dr Wilcox,' he told her. 'I'm in the village—haven't I seen you in church?'

'Yes, Mrs Pearson's my aunt.'

He gave her back her hand. 'Well, your pulse is all right. Get as warm as you can, quickly.'

'Will Peggy be all right?'

'I think so—we'll know for sure when she's been seen by a specialist.'

He went away and Lady Trueman said, 'My dear, you must forgive us—it was such a shock. Bessy shall help you—a hot bath and then a quiet rest by the fire while your clothes dry. I'll phone your aunt.' She added worriedly, 'I do hope this specialist will come soon...'

Bessy came then, and led Margo away to help her out of her wet clothes and to run a hot bath, fragrant with bath essence. Margo sank into it thankfully.

She would have fallen asleep if Bessy hadn't come to rouse her.

'Your clothes are being dried, miss. If you'll get out I'll give you a good rub down and there's a warm blanket to wrap you in.'

'The specialist isn't here yet?'

'Like as not he'll come from London—take him best part of an hour or more, even if he started off the moment he got Dr Wilcox's message. He's here still, waiting for him.'

Swathed in a soft blanket, Margo was led back to the nursery and seated by the fire, and presently Bessy brought her a glass of milk.

'There's a drop of brandy in it, miss, to ward off the chill. Why don't you close your eyes for a few minutes? Lady Trueman's phoned your aunt and you'll be taken home as soon as your clothes are dry. There's only one shoe...'

'I lost the other in the stream. It doesn't matter.' Margo took the glass. 'Thank you for the milk, Bessy, and all your help.'

There must have been more than a drop of brandy, for Margo, nicely warm again, dozed off. She didn't hear the arrival of the specialist, who examined Peggy at some length, conferred with Dr Wilcox and then prepared to take his leave. He was standing having a last word with him when Dr Wilcox said, 'The young lady who found the child and carried her in is still here. She had a soaking and a tiring walk carrying Peggy. I took a quick look at her but...'

'You would like me to cast an eye over her?'

'I believe Lady Trueman would like that—just in case there is further damage.'

'Just so.'

The two men trod into the nursery and Margo opened a sleepy eye.

Professor van Kessel eyed her with a faint smile. 'It seems that we are destined only to meet in emergencies, Margo.'

CHAPTER THREE

MARGO blinked, her delight at the sight of him doused by the knowledge that she looked even worse than usual, cocooned in a blanket with her hair still damp. And probably, she thought miserably, the brandy had given her a red nose.

Indeed it had—contrasting strongly with her still pale face. The professor, looking at her, found himself wondering why he was pleased to see her again. He had thought about her from time to time, this plain, rather bossy girl. A typical vicar's daughter, but one, he had to admit to himself, who would keep her head in an emergency and use the common sense she had so obviously been endowed with. Not, he had thought, the kind of girl he would want to spend an evening with. Now he wasn't so sure. There was more to Margo than met the eye...

'Is Peggy going to be all right?' She had wriggled upright in her chair, nothing visible but her face and a great deal of untidy hair.

'I think so; she is regaining consciousness. We'll have her X-rayed in the morning. What about you, Margo?'

'Me? I'm fine; I just got a bit wet.'

He turned easily to Dr Wilcox. 'Margo and I have met before on occasion. I certainly didn't expect to see her here.'

'She's not staying with Lady Trueman; she's visiting her aunt, Mrs Pearson, who lives in the village.' Dr

Wilcox smiled at Margo. 'I'll pop in tomorrow and see that you are none the worse for your soaking—'

He broke off as Bessy came in. 'Didn't know anyone was here,' she excused herself. 'I've brought Miss Pearson's clothes. Lady Trueman says as soon as she's ready she'll be driven back to her aunt's place.'

'Ah, well, as to that,' observed the professor mildly, 'by the time Dr Wilcox and I have had a little chat with Peggy's mother, Miss Pearson will be ready to leave. I can give her a lift on my way.'

Dr Wilcox gave him a quick glance. He had known the professor for some years—had met him at seminars, read his learned articles in the medical journals, and got to know him even better at a convention in Leiden. He admired him and knew that he was highly regarded in his profession—knew him to be a reserved man, whose private life was, as far as he was concerned, private. The last man, he would have thought, to show more than a courteous interest in the small pale girl wrapped in that blanket. They already knew each other, though. He must tell his wife when he got home.

Now he said cheerfully, 'Oh, splendid. Miss Pearson will be glad to get back to her aunt.'

He's just being polite, Margo told herself as she got back into her dry but hopelessly crushed clothes. It was no good putting on just one shoe. She was wondering what to do about that when Lady Trueman came in.

'My dear Margo, how shockingly we have treated you. Do forgive us—it has been such a shock. You are sure you are able to go back to your aunt? Bessy tells me that the professor has offered to take you home. So good of him. What a reassuring man he is—Peggy is conscious again and is to be X-rayed in the morning, and he will visit again when he has seen the result.

When I think of that child lying there! We can never thank you enough…' Lady Trueman paused for breath.

'Had she run away from her nanny?'

Lady Trueman's pleasant face became quite ferocious.

'That woman. She is to leave immediately. She had left Peggy playing alone in the gardens while she went to chat with one of the gardeners. Do you know, she was still there when you came back? And never once gave a thought to Peggy? I told Helen when she engaged her that she was far too young and flighty…

'Lord Trueman will most certainly wish to thank you when he gets back home…'

Bessy peered round the door. 'The professor's ready to leave, my lady. I was to tell you and Miss Pearson.'

He was in the hall with Dr Wilcox and Helen, and Margo, very conscious of her stockinged feet, padded across the icy, marble-paved floor. It was the professor who came to meet her. He swallowed a desire to laugh at her ramshackle appearance.

'If someone could let Miss Pearson have a pair of shoes—boots—anything…'

It was Bessy who asked what size her feet were and sped away to return in a moment with a pair of wellies. 'Better than nothing,' she muttered.

'Of course we'll replace your shoes, Margo,' said Helen, and took her hand. 'We are so grateful.'

She began to cry again.

A pretty little woman, reflected the professor, but lacking common sense—utterly dependent on everyone else. He wasn't aware that he was comparing her with Margo.

With perfect good manners he got himself and her out of the house, popped her into the car and drove away.

'Will you tell me where your aunt lives? Close by, I gather.'

'The first house on the left when you reach the village in about two minutes. How did you get here? I mean, do you live close by?'

'Fairly near. Tell me, Margo, do you spend your life coping with emergencies? And why are you so far from home?'

He hadn't answered her question; she shouldn't have asked it in the first place. She sneezed. 'I'm visiting my aunt—father's sister-in-law. She's an archdeacon's widow.'

'You spring from an ecclesiastic family—and yet you intend to be a farmer's wife?'

She sneezed again, and he passed her a very large white handkerchief.

'No, I don't. I told George I didn't want to marry him. He hadn't exactly asked me, but I thought I'd tell him first and save him the trouble.'

He turned a laugh into a cough. 'How very sensible of you. I must admit that I find it hard to imagine you as a farmer's wife.'

'Well, I dare say you do. I expect you think of me as a vicar's daughter.' She spoke without rancour. 'That's my aunt's house on the left. Thank you for the lift; it was most kind...'

All he said was, 'Stay where you are.' And he got out of the car and opened her door, waiting patiently while she sneezed yet again.

'That's going to be a nasty cold. I think I should see your aunt.'

Mrs Pearson opened the door as they reached it.

'Dear child, come inside at once.'

As she ushered them into the sitting room she cast an eye over the professor and he said smoothly, 'Mrs

Pearson? I was called in to see Peggy and have brought Margo back to you. Strangely enough, we have met before. Dr Wilcox will call tomorrow and take a look at Margo, but in the meantime perhaps I might advise that she be put to bed at once. Warm drinks and a quiet day in the house tomorrow. I'm afraid she has caught a cold.' He smiled at her. 'Gijs van Kessel.'

Mrs Pearson liked the look of him, and she liked the sound of his quiet, assured voice. She held out a hand. 'Can you spare the time to tell me exactly what has happened? I had a very garbled version over the phone.'

'Certainly, Mrs Pearson. You will want to get Margo to bed at once, will you not?' He looked at Margo. Bed was undoubtedly the best place for her. 'If I might suggest another hot drink and two aspirins? A good night's sleep will put things to rights again.'

Margo peered at him from watery eyes and sniffed from a stuffed-up nose. Nothing, she had discovered at that very moment, could be put to rights again. Life would never be the same again either. How could it be? The peculiar feeling she had been experiencing for the last hour or so wasn't a cold in the head, it was love! And to have fallen in love so completely with a man who looked at her with kind detachment and not a vestige of interest in her as a person was ridiculous, and she must put a stop to it immediately.

She said, as briskly as another sneeze permitted, 'Thank you for bringing me back, Professor. There's really nothing wrong with me; I shall be fine in the morning.' She held out a hand. 'Goodbye.'

He took the hand—small, nicely shaped and capable—and held it fast.

'Not goodbye, Margo. I feel sure that we shall meet again.'

She looked up into his face and saw kindness there. There was something else too—amusement?

She took her hand away smartly. 'Perhaps.'

At the door she said, 'I'm quite all right to put myself to bed, Aunt Flo. I'll get some aspirins and milk as I go.'

Her aunt nodded. 'Very well, child. I'll pop in and see you later on. A little light supper, perhaps?'

She closed the door firmly after her niece. 'Do sit down,' she bade the professor. 'Margo will be all right; she's very healthy and strong.'

'It might be wise to keep her in bed until Dr Wilcox sees her tomorrow. It wasn't only getting so wet; she carried the child for quite a distance, and with only one shoe on—moreover, she was afraid for Peggy's life. She acted with great good sense.'

'Something she has always possessed in abundance. Lady Trueman was full of praise for her conduct!' Aunt Florence settled herself more comfortably in her chair. 'There'll be coffee in a moment, or would you prefer a drink?'

'Coffee would be delightful. Is Margo staying with you for some time?'

'Another week or so. You said you had met her already—at her home?'

'Yes. Actually we first met on a lonely road in the middle of the night...' He told his hostess about it very simply. 'And since then I have been to her home,' he concluded.

Aunt Florence poured the coffee. 'Oh, then you'll know all about George. I must say I was very relieved to hear that she has decided not to marry him. They have known each other for years and it was a gradual thing, you know—his mother liked the idea, thought that Margo could be moulded into the kind of wife she wanted for George. Only Margo isn't a girl one can mould. There was no engagement—indeed, she tells me that he had never actually asked her to marry him and took it all in good part. I shall be sorry for his wife when he does marry—his mother, you know.'

'So now Margo can rearrange her future to suit herself?' The professor spoke idly.

'Well, as to that, she has had no training of any sort. An excellent education, but she has been at home for several years.' She added severely, 'Margo is a good daughter. It is to be hoped that she will get the chance to be a good wife and mother.'

The professor murmured politely, drank his coffee and presently took his leave. He had interrupted a free day—a rare occurrence—in order to confer with Dr Wilcox, and now he wanted to get back to the quiet evening he had planned.

He had been surprised to see Margo again; she tended to pop up in the most unexpected places. She hadn't shown any particular pleasure at seeing him once more—although, he reflected, he had been pleased as well as surprised to see her.

He couldn't think why; she had no looks to speak of, her nose had been red and she had sniffed a good deal! And she had never made the slightest attempt to attract his attention. He remembered briefly the considerable number of women who had done just the opposite. Perhaps that was why he liked her. She obviously didn't mind in the least what his opinion of her was and he was sure that if she thought he should be put in his place then that was exactly what she would do.

He smiled at the idea and decided that when he went back to see Peggy, after the X-rays had been taken, he would call at Mrs Pearson's and see how Margo did.

His decision set at rest a vague feeling of disquiet.

He wouldn't like her to be ill. She was young and healthy and clearly not given to making the worst of things. All the same she had put him in mind of a half-drowned kitten he had once rescued...

Margo, much refreshed by a brief nap, ate the splendid supper her aunt brought to her later that evening, swallowed more aspirins and went to sleep again, to wake in the morning feeling quite herself but with a streaming cold.

'You'll stay where you are until Dr Wilcox has been,' ordered Aunt Flo, at her most stern. 'Now just lie back, dear, while I rub your chest with camphorated oil.'

Margo did as she was told—people seldom disobeyed Aunt Flo—and presently, much soothed by the old-fashioned remedy, she lay back on her pillows, reeking of camphor, quite happy to do nothing more energetic than blow her small red nose at intervals.

She was sipping more hot milk when Dr Wilcox called and, escorted by Aunt Flo, entered the bedroom—to recoil at the overpowering atmosphere.

'Camphorated oil,' said Aunt Flo, in a voice which dared him to say anything detrimental about it.

'A splendid old-fashioned remedy—very soothing to the patient,' agreed the doctor.

He took a quick look at Margo and pronounced her none the worse for her wetting, but advised that she spend the rest of the day in bed. 'Paracetamol every four hours and drink all you can. There's no need for me to call again unless you're anxious about anything.'

'Is Peggy better?'

'Yes. No great harm done. Concussion and a nasty bruise. I saw the X-rays. She's to stay in bed for a few days, though.'

He got off the bed. 'Lady Trueman is coming to visit you in a day or two, when your cold is better. She is so very grateful. It could have been much worse but for your prompt action.'

He shook hands and went away and Aunt Flo returned with a bouquet of flowers in Cellophane, tied with a great deal of ribbon. 'These have just come. There's a card...'

Margo read the card. They were from the Truemans and Helen. The thought that they might have been from the professor was absurd, to be dismissed at once. She said brightly, 'Aren't they beautiful? Will you keep them in the sitting room, Aunt? There are so many of them, and I'll be downstairs tomorrow.'

Excepting her thickened speech and a constantly blown nose, Margo was indeed quite herself by the following morning. She was dusting the numerous knick-knacks in her aunt's sitting room when the professor called.

She hadn't expected him, although she had been thinking about him, and the sudden sight of him sent the colour into her cheeks.

'Entertain him while I see about coffee,' commanded Aunt Flo, and went away.

Margo put down the hideous Victorian vase she was holding. 'Hello,' she said. 'Have you been to see Peggy?'

'I've seen her; now I've come to see you.' He smiled gently.

'Oh, yes, well, do sit down.' She picked up a delicate Spode bowl and began to dust it. 'I hope she's better?'

'Going along nicely. And you, Margo?'

'Me? Oh, I'm quite well, thank you.' She very much wanted to blow her nose, but gave a surreptitious sniff instead.

He was sitting very much at his ease, looking at her, making no further attempt to speak. He could at least make an effort, she thought crossly. Her pretty colour had faded, leaving her pale, with puffed eyelids and a pink nose. Aware of this, she said peevishly, 'Haven't you any other patients to see?'

He said placidly, 'Oh, yes, quite a few—but not until this afternoon. A clinic at the hospital...'

'Children?'

'Scores of them—crying and being sick and wetting themselves. They will all be ill, though.'

'So you don't mind if they are tiresome?'

'No. Would you like to come and see them one day?'

'May I? Although I don't go to London very often...'

'Oh, I'd pick you up and bring you back. It would make a good subject next time you have a get-together at the village hall.'

She looked at him to make sure that he wasn't joking. He wasn't.

'Well, yes. There's the Mothers' Union and the WI, and some of the older children from the Sunday School...'

She smiled at him. He wasn't only the man she had fallen in love with, he was a man to admire and trust and be perfectly safe with. Her eyes sparkled and glowed in her face so that he didn't see the red nose and the puffy eyelids any longer, only the gentle curve of her mouth and her sweet smile.

Aunt Florence came in then, and they drank their coffee and talked about the weather and the excellent apple crop and the still distant approach of Christmas.

'November already,' observed Aunt Florence. 'Let us hope that we have a period of good weather... Do you return to your home for Christmas, Professor?'

'Oh, yes. I'm only here for another month or so.'

Just as well, thought Margo; then I can forget him. It took all her common sense to dispel the wave of sadness which engulfed her person.

The same common sense prompted her to empty her head of him once he had bade them goodbye and driven away and plunge into preparations for the church bazaar, the committee of which was chaired by Aunt Flo.

'You couldn't have been here at a better time,' that lady told her, sorting through the piles of contributions for the stalls, housed for the moment in the box-room. 'You will have a stall, of course, dear—good-as-new clothes.'

Margo said dutifully, 'Yes, Aunt. Do people really buy other people's clothes?'

'Good gracious me, yes. Lady Trueman's hats are very popular, and that young woman who works for the BBC and lives at the other end of the village—she has sent some really very nice things. Farmer Deadman's youngest is marrying in the spring; I've on doubt she'll snap up some of the dresses—just right for a wedding—and there's a lovely dressing gown—you know, one of those loose, flowing ones.

'Pass me my pen, dear, and I'll start pricing some of these things. You can fold them up and put them in those boxes ready to take down to the hall in the morning.'

Several days of hard work ensued. Aunt Florence, who Margo decided must have been a regimental sergeant major in some former life, marshalled her helpers, willing and unwilling, and saw to it that no one slacked. To give her her due, by Saturday afternoon, with the stalls stocked, the hall decorated and somebody at the door ready to take the entrance fee, she had achieved everything she had promised the committee she would do.

Margo, arranging the last few clothes, could hear the voices of the small queue already outside the door, which was due to be opened at any moment now. She rearranged the looking glass just so, so that the prospective purchasers could view their chosen articles in comfort, and took a quick look to make sure that her nose, still faintly pink from her cold, wasn't shining.

The door was opened and a great many people surged in, impatient to start looking for bargains but having to wait while Lady Trueman—just arrived in her car—made her usual speech and declared the bazaar open. The rector spoke too, but experience had taught him to make it very brief; his audience were already heading towards the particular stalls they fancied.

Margo did a brisk trade. It was fortunate that some of the things left from several years ago—rejects from bygone bazaars—were, as Aunt Flo observed, quite in style again, fashion being what it was.

The newer clothes went fast too. She had hung them in sizes, which helped a bit but didn't prevent a good deal of impulse-buying which she knew would be regretted later. She was helping an elderly woman choose a hat when she glanced up and saw Professor van Kessel, quite close by, watching her.

She offered the lady a feather toque, and he shook his head slightly and came nearer.

'The brown one with the brim,' he suggested, and smiled at her customer, who, taken by surprise, removed the toque and poised the hat of his choice on her grey hair.

'Well, dearie me, love, the gentleman's quite right. It suits me a treat. How much?'

'Seventy-five pence. A real bargain and just right for you—smart, too.'

'For me grandson's wedding, New Year's Day.' She

beamed at the professor. 'Thank you kindly, sir. Got a wife of your own, I dare say, to choose hats for!'

'I'm sure you will look very nice in it.' He smiled his kind smile and she took the hat in the bag Margo had found for it and trotted off.

He said then belatedly, 'Hello, Margo.' He glanced round. 'A pity there is nothing here which I can buy.'

'However did you get here?'

'In my car,' he said, and when she frowned added, 'I had a last visit to pay to Peggy.'

He glanced round him at the women inspecting the clothes on the stall. 'When will you be free?'

'We stay open till half past five and then we clear up.'

He nodded. 'From the look of things, you won't have much to clear up on this stall. Have you seen Lady Trueman?'

'Well, no. She doesn't stay. A lot of people don't come. I mean it's their hats and clothes, if you understand me.'

'Ah, of course. I'm just going to have a word with someone...'

He wandered away, and a moment later she saw him bending his height to speak to Helen and presently joining her to go to the other end of the hall.

How strange it is, mused Margo, that we meet whenever I'm looking a fright or doing something quite unglamorous. She became so lost in thought about this that she sold a size fourteen dress to a size eighteen woman without noticing. Out of the corner of her eye she could see him still with Helen, laughing with her. It didn't seem quite fair. After all, Helen had already got a husband; she had lovely clothes too, and a pretty face.

Margo, ashamed of her thoughts, allowed a pert

young woman from the new estate in the next village to buy the last two hats at a very reduced price. The stall was almost empty now. A hard core of dresses, obviously bought by mistake in the first place, hung limply on their hangers; they would be bundled up once again and reappear at the spring jumble sale in aid of church funds.

She was folding the last of them—puce nylon with a pattern of startling green leaves and a draped front guaranteed to disguise the wearer's curves completely—when the professor returned to the stall.

'Finished? Good. How long will you be?'

'Half an hour or so—why?'

'I thought we might have dinner. Your aunt tells me that she is invited out for drinks and will probably be asked to dine with these friends of hers.'

Margo gave him a thoughtful look. 'Thank you, but I've several things to do this evening and I can get my own supper if Aunt Florence isn't there.'

'Ah, you think—mistakenly—that I am obliging her by taking you out for a meal. Nothing of the kind. I consider it high time that we spent an hour or so in each other's company unhampered by emergencies of any sort.'

'Why?'

'I think that if we had time to talk we might find that we have quite a lot in common.'

She had made up her mind not to see him again, to forget him, to pretend that they had never met, and above all to convince herself that she didn't love him... 'All right,' she said, promising herself silently that it was just this once.

'I'll come for you in about an hour,' he told her, and went away to talk to the rector.

Margo totted up her takings, put the discarded

dresses back in their box and went in search of her aunt, who, apprised of her plans, nodded her approval.

'Go back to the house as soon as you're ready, child. I'll be home presently. You had better take a key with you. Where are you going?'

'I don't know.'

'Wear your blue dress…'

Margo agreed. She had no option; it was the only suitable garment she had. A pretty colour, and nicely cut, it was nevertheless hardly a garment to inspire a man to give it, or her, a second glance. It was all she had though…

Margo peered at her person in her aunt's pier glass and decided that she would do. She did her hair with extra care, applied lipstick and powder and, encouraged by the result, went downstairs to find the professor chatting to her aunt.

He greeted her with easy friendliness, told her in just the right tone of voice that she looked nice and thought what a pity it was that her clothes were so dull. A pity, indeed; she had a pretty figure and nice legs and she deserved better than the uninspired dress she was wearing.

He took her to the Oakley Court Hotel at Windsor—a country house hotel, with grounds running down to the river, and inside a pleasant cosiness combined with charming surroundings and excellent food.

Gijs hadn't bothered to think why he wanted Margo to have an evening out with him, but when he had seen her that afternoon, surrounded by cast-off hats and out-of-date dresses, he had a wish to take her away from it all, to find out what she was really like, what she wanted from life, if she was content…

They had a drink at the bar before going to their candlelit table in the restaurant. Margo glanced round her as they sat down. The dress was all wrong but there was nothing she could do about that, and since she was sitting down no one could see that it was the wrong length too. She dismissed it from her mind and studied the menu.

Spinach tartlets, then roast duck with cherry sauce, game chips and braised celery, followed by a lemon soufflé, accompanied by a bottle of Nuits St Georges, served to put Margo at her ease; never mind the dress, she was with Gijs, eating a delicious meal and drinking wine which tasted quite different from the occasional bottle she'd chosen from the supermarkets for birthdays and Christmas. She began to enjoy herself.

The professor had no difficulty in leading her on to talk about herself. He was aware that normally that was something she wouldn't do, but the wine had loosened her tongue and she answered his gently put questions readily enough.

'You do not wish for a career?' he asked casually.

'Well, I'm too old to start, aren't I?' she observed matter-of-factly. 'I would have liked to have travelled after I left school—just to Europe to have a look round—and I think that I would have enjoyed nursing…'

'You do not regret giving up George?'

'Not a bit.' She chose a chocolate from the dish which had come with the coffee.

'Would you like to marry?'

'Oh, yes, but I don't think too much about that because I don't think it's very likely.'

'Why not?'

She kept her voice light. 'I have no looks. If I had a fortune perhaps it would help—and lovely clothes!' She frowned at him across the table. 'I'm talking far too much. Not that it matters. I mean, you're a doctor and that's almost like talking to a man of the church, isn't it? Besides, we're unlikely to see each other again.'

'When we do meet each other it is on the most unlikely occasions.'

'You're going back to Holland soon. Will you be pleased to go?'

'It is my country. I shall always have one foot in England, though—I have consultancy posts at several hospitals here. I go wherever I'm needed, but Holland is my home.'

She longed to ask him about his life there, but something in his manner stopped her. Besides, she reflected, the less she knew about him, the easier it would be to forget him. She began to talk about the bazaar and the small events in the village, and presently he drove her back to Aunt Florence's house and when she thanked him for her evening told her quietly that he had enjoyed it too. He didn't say that he wanted to see her again before he went back to Holland, nor did he ask her when she was going back home.

'What did you expect?' She asked her reflection in the old-fashioned dressing-table mirror in her bedroom as she got ready for bed. And, although not a girl to cry easily, she cried herself to sleep.

During the next few days she saw something of Helen. Invited to tea, she made friends with Peggy—still in her bed and with a new nanny in charge.

'She's almost well again now,' said Helen. 'Such a relief. I have never been so scared in my whole life. Thank heaven that you found her, Margo, and that Dr Wilcox was able to get hold of that marvellous specialist. Didn't you think he was gorgeous? He's not married. I asked him, and when he said he wasn't I told him that he ought to get himself a wife. I mean people expect it, don't they?' She waved a hand. 'You know, specialist in children's illness and so on—it would make him even more dependable, if you see what I mean.'

'If he's already well-known I don't suppose it matters much.'

'Wait until you're married and have children; you'll know what I mean.' Helen bit her lip. Margo's chances of marrying seemed to her to be a bit slight.

Margo was to go back home. Her father would drive up in the car and she would go back to the gentle, monotonous routine of her daily life at Thinbottom.

She packed her bag, made her aunt a present of a particular rose bush she had coveted and laid the table for lunch while Phoebe made a casserole.

'You must not travel on empty stomachs,' declared Aunt Flo. 'Put out the coffee-cups, Margo, and go to the kitchen and make sure the coffee's ready, with a plate of Phoebe's biscuits.'

Margo heard the front doorbell while she was warming the milk.

'I'd better take the tray in,' she told Phoebe. 'That must be Father...'

It was the professor, standing before the fire, talking to her aunt.

She put the tray down carefully, her heart in her throat, choking her. Here he was again, and in no time at all she would be gone.

'I'll fetch another cup,' she said, and smiled vaguely in his general direction.

'No need, Margo,' declared Aunt Florence. 'Gijs will drive you back—I quite forgot to tell you that he phoned yesterday evening to say that he was going your way and wanting to know if you would like a lift. I phoned your father.'

Aunt Florence spoke with her usual certainty that any arrangement she might choose to make was agreeable to everyone else. 'Pour the coffee, dear.'

So Margo poured the coffee and handed out cups and biscuits and answered politely when spoken to. It was hard, she reflected, that, having made up her mind to forget him, he should turn up again. She took care not to look at him, and presently said that she thought she would go to the kitchen and give Phoebe a hand.

'No need,' said her aunt. 'I want you to run down to the rectory with the accounts for the bazaar; I promised the rector I would let him have them today. Gijs can go with you—I dare say he'd like to stretch his legs.'

So Margo got into her jacket, wound a scarf round her small neck and declared herself ready. Going down the garden path, she said awkwardly, 'I'm sorry about this. I dare say you want to leave as quickly as possible, and really there was no need for you to come with me.'

'Why should I wish to hurry away? I have been invited to lunch. Why do you take it for granted that I don't wish to be with you, Margo? You really must cultivate a better opinion of yourself. Are you not pleased to see me?'

'Yes, of course. I was a bit surprised.' She kept her voice steady and looked up into his face. 'I'm always pleased to see you, only each time I do I expect it to be the last.'

He tucked her hand under his arm. 'Next week I'm coming down to Thinbottom to take you to the hospital as I promised. You can spend the day there and I'll bring you back in the evening.'

'You will?' Her eyes sparkled. 'I'll love that. Which day?'

'Tuesday—you will have to be ready quite early in the morning.'

'Oh, I will. Here's the rectory...'

They were both invited in, and while one of the children went to fetch his father his wife led them into the sitting room.

'Do sit down,' she invited. She was a gossipy little woman, wanting to hear the details of Peggy's accident firsthand.

'So romantic,' she cried. 'And you two knowing each other and meeting again at Lord Trueman's. You must both...'

Luckily they were spared the rest because the rector joined them at that moment. A good thing, too, for Margo's cheeks had pinkened and the professor's features had assumed a blandness which she was sure hid amusement.

On the way back she said, 'I'm sorry about that...'

He took her arm. 'Why? It must appear romantic to those who don't know us. After all, how are they to know that neither of us has any interest in romance?'

She had no answer to that.

CHAPTER FOUR

IT WAS obvious that Aunt Florence approved of the professor. Over the casserole and the treacle tart which followed it the talk was leisurely and covered any number of subjects. It was only when he glanced at his watch and observed that they should be going that Aunt Florence got up reluctantly from the table.

Bidding them goodbye presently, she said, 'I hope I shall see you—both of you—again soon. Margo knows that she is always welcome—and you, Gijs, if you are so inclined—although I dare say you are a very busy man and have any number of friends.'

She stood in the doorway, watching them get into the Rolls. Margo had been unusually quiet during lunch, she reflected. Probably a little sad at the thought of the mundane life she was returning to. She and the professor seemed to get on well enough—a casual friendliness which Aunt Flo supposed was all that could be expected from two people who lived such different lives. She watched the car until it was out of sight then went back indoors, feeling lonely; Margo had been a pleasant companion, someone nice to have around the house.

Professor van Kessel was thinking much the same thing as he talked casually about nothing in particular. He sensed that Margo was ill at ease and was intent on finding out why.

She sat very still beside him, looking out of the window and making suitable replies in her pretty voice, but she made no effort to start any conversation.

'You're sorry to be going back home?' he asked.

'No, of course not. I've had a lovely holiday, though.'

He remembered the bazaar, and wondered if staying with Aunt Florence had been very much different from being at home. He thought not. Sunday School, Mothers' Union, arranging flowers, visiting parishioners and arranging whist drives, though splendidly worthwhile tasks in themselves, weren't enough to fill a girl's life. Not a girl like Margo, he reflected, who would make a splendid wife and mother. He must contrive to let her meet some of the younger doctors at the hospital on Tuesday.

They arrived back in time for a late tea but he didn't stay for that. He made his excuses with his beautiful manners, giving no reason for his refusal, bade them goodbye, reminded Margo to be ready on Tuesday and drove away.

'I dare say he's on his way to a hospital or a meeting,' observed Mrs Pearson. 'A pity he couldn't stay for tea.' She brightened. 'Perhaps he's having it with friends. Nice of him to give you a lift, love.'

Margo agreed. Well, it had been nice of him, and after all that was all it had been—a lift home because he happened to be going that way too. Not, she told herself firmly, because he enjoyed her company.

There was Tuesday, of course, but she had no doubt that once they were at the hospital she would see nothing of him—probably he regretted his invitation. She should have refused...

It seemed a month of Sundays until Tuesday. In reality it was only a few days away, and those days were fully occupied: driving her father to Blandford, shopping for her mother, sitting in on the committee planning Christmas entertainment for the Sunday School.

It came at last and she stood ready and waiting at half past eight in the morning, sure that he had forgotten.

He arrived exactly when he had said he would, accepted the coffee her mother had ready, then stowed her into the car and began the drive back to London.

'You must have got up very early,' observed Margo. 'I hope you had a good night's sleep.'

He assured her that he had, touched by her concern.

'The colleague I am staying with is an old friend and a most considerate host, but I intend to look around for a small house in London. I come here so frequently nowadays—sometimes for a couple of days, sometimes for weeks at a time.'

'But you have a home in Holland?'

'Oh, yes.'

That was all he would tell her.

'I'm handing you over to one of the housemen at the hospital; he'll take you round and then bring you to my clinic. Alec Jackson—I think you will like him. He has an excellent future ahead of him.' He glanced sideways at her serene profile. 'I'll drive you back some time this evening—I can't be certain when.'

'I'm sure I'm going to enjoy every minute,' she assured him. Even if she didn't see him again at the hospital there was the drive back home to look forward to...

The hospital was in the East End, crammed in amongst narrow streets of small houses and down-at-heel shops. Margo, seeing it for the first time, felt some disappointment at the sight of its elaborate Victorian brickwork and narrow windows, but, once urged inside by the professor, saw that the aspect was quite different: light walls, bright pictures, plenty of lights and potted plants, and as a background to these a steady tide of noise, rising and falling and never ceasing.

The entrance hall was quite small, with corridors leading away from it in all directions. The professor glanced at his watch and Margo saw his faint frown, but his face cleared as a young man came hurrying to meet them.

'Good morning, sir.' He had a cheerful, blunt-featured face, and smiled at her as the professor spoke.

'Good morning, Jackson; this is Margo Pearson. Take her everywhere and take care of her for me. When she's seen all she wishes to see, bring her along to the clinic, will you?'

He smiled down at Margo. 'I hope you enjoy your visit,' he said, and didn't wait for her answer but strode away.

'He's got a busy day ahead of him,' said Alex Jackson. 'Running a bit late already.' He touched her arm. 'We'll have coffee first, if you like, in the canteen, while I explain the lay-out of the place. It's like a rabbit warren.'

The canteen was half-full, but they found a table and sat down facing each other. 'May I call you Margo?' asked Alex. 'Have you known the professor for a long time?'

'No—a month or so. And I don't know him well, only we've met from time to time and he suggested I might like to see the hospital. Do you work for him?'

'I'm on his team—very junior, I must add. He's a splendid man—marvellous with children. There's this op he does to lengthen malformed legs—very complicated. There are a couple of patients here who have had it done; you'll see them presently.' He added, 'If you want to powder your nose the Ladies' is over there. I'll wait for you here.'

You couldn't help but like him, thought Margo as she was whisked from one ward to the next. She would have liked a brother like him, someone she could talk to and laugh with.

True to his promise, he showed her two small boys, each with a leg encased in steel rods and bars with screws at one side.

'They have to be turned once a day,' explained Alec, and at her look hastened to add that it didn't hurt a bit. 'Not feeling squeamish, are you?' he wanted to know anxiously. 'The professor said you never turned a hair under any circumstances.'

'Did he? No, I'm not squeamish, Alec, and it's a marvellous thing to be able to do, isn't it? He must be very clever. Do you operate?'

Alec looked pleased at her question. 'Minor stuff—and I take my turn at scrubbing to assist.'

'So one day you will be like Professor van Kessel?'

'Can't hope to reach his heights, but I'll have a go at any rate. Come and see the prem ward then we'll go and get something to eat before we go to the clinic.'

They ate beefburgers and chips and jam roly-poly pudding while Alex talked and she listened. They were firm friends by now, enjoying each other's company.

Margo, absorbing information the way a sponge absorbed water, was a pleasant surprise to Alec. He had undertaken to escort Margo when the professor had asked him, resigned to a boring day, but she had turned out to be both intelligent and interested. A great girl, he reflected; never mind her plain face. And when she looked at you her eyes were magnificent...

The clinic was still crowded and very noisy. There was a short corridor at the far end, with doors on either side, and a constant flow of people going to and fro along it.

'The consulting rooms,' explained Alex. 'The professor's got the first one on this side, then there's his registrar and the junior registrar and two more doctors at the end. The professor sees all the new patients and the serious cases, and also any of the children his team refer to him.'

'But there must be hundreds here.'

'Something like that—it seems more with all the screeching and bawling.'

'I wish I could see him working…'

'More than my life's worth. There he is now, going along to see a child in the junior registrar's room.'

Margo craned her neck. He looked different in a long white coat, with a stethoscope slung around his shoulders and a fistful of papers in one hand.

'He looks so clever,' she observed in a whisper.

'Well, he is.' Alex smiled at her. 'He'll come back presently; you'll be able to see him better then.'

When he did return the professor saw them at once, standing to one side. Alex was saying something to Margo, who was smiling at him. They appeared to be on excellent terms. The professor frowned, feeling no pleasure at the sight, quite forgetting that the whole idea of bringing Margo to the hospital was so that she might meet one or two young men…

The pair of them stayed for some time, and then, when there was a mere handful of patients left, went back to the canteen once more to drink strong tea and eat currant buns.

'You should train as a nurse,' suggested Alec. 'A children's nurse.'

'I'm too old,' said Margo matter-of-factly. 'I'm twenty-eight. Besides, I'm quite busy at home. It's only a small village but there's always something…'

'You're not too old. You don't look as though you're

twenty-eight either,' observed Alex generously. He added with a burst of candour, 'The professor said you were a sensible girl, with no silly ideas, and I expected a kind of schoolteacher type, if you know what I mean. You're not a bit like that—just the opposite. I dare say he was comparing you with some of his elegant lady-friends.'

Margo laughed with him, inwardly boiling with rage. How dared the professor describe her as a school-teacher, and a sensible one too? If she didn't love him so much she would hate him. If that's what he thinks of me then I'll be just that, she told herself. Just let him wait until he drives me home.

Alec, unaware of the feelings he had stirred up be-hind Margo's pleasant little face, was on the point of suggesting that they might meet again when his phone bleeped.

'The professor is waiting for us.'

Margo pondered the idea of having another cup of tea and keeping him waiting, but that might get Alec into trouble. She followed him out, outwardly meek, back through the hospital to the front entrance, and found the professor leaning against a wall reading the porter's evening paper. He handed it back as they reached him, expressed the hope that they had had a satisfactory day, and held the door open for Margo.

'Thanks, Alec,' he said, and listened while he was told that their tour had been most enjoyable. Then he watched as Margo shook hands with Alec and echoed his wish that they might meet again soon. She knew it was not at all likely, but even schoolteacher types had their moments!

She smiled very sweetly at Alec. 'It was lovely,' she reiterated, with a show of warmth especially for the professor's benefit. 'You made it all so interesting...'

She got into the car then, turning to wave as they drove away and then sitting as still as a mouse.

Presently the professor asked, 'So the day was a success? Alec gave you lunch?'

'Yes, thank you.'

He tried again. 'What did you enjoy most?'

She thought before she replied. 'The two boys whose legs were being lengthened. Their little faces and their cheerful acceptance of having their legs in those awful contraptions. And knowing that later on they will be normal, like other boys.'

Her voice was cool but she was still boiling away inside, and he was quick to sense that.

'What is the matter, Margo?'

'Matter? There is nothing the matter, Professor.'

'You would prefer not to talk?'

'Yes.' Such a small word, he thought, and fired like a bullet from a gun. Something had upset her and he wondered what it was. Not Alec, surely? They had parted the best of friends—indeed, with the promise of future meetings. Which was exactly what he had hoped for, wasn't it?

Conversation languished after that, Margo's polite and chilly replies bringing each topic he introduced to a dead end. Only when they reached the vicarage and he stopped before its door did he turn to her.

'I wish to know what has upset you, Margo.'

'Nothing. I'm not upset,' she told him stonily.

'We will sit here until you tell me.'

As she put a hand on the door he reached over and put it gently back into her lap. 'Well?'

She looked at him then. 'You said I was a sensible girl with no silly ideas; Alec thought I sounded like a schoolteacher. If that's what you think of me I don't want to see you again, ever.'

'But you *are* a sensible girl, and to the best of my knowledge refreshingly lacking in silly ideas...'

'There, you see what I mean? It's called damning with faint praise. Now I'm going in. Thank you for letting me visit the hospital.'

She put a hand on the door and this time he didn't stop her, but got out too and walked with her to the front door, where she asked him in a voice straight from the deep freeze if he would care for a cup of coffee.

'In the circumstances, no, Margo.'

He sounded as though he was laughing, and she said fiercely, 'Oh, I hope I never see you again!'

He didn't answer that but got back into the car, and was driving away as her mother opened the door.

'Darling—but Gijs is going? Can't he stop for a cup of coffee or supper?'

Margo stepped into the warmth of the hall and shut the door behind her.

'No, he couldn't stop. He's a very busy man, Mother. Wait while I take off my things and I'll tell you about my day—it was fascinating...'

When she had finished her mother remarked, 'You didn't see much of Gijs, then?'

'Only from a distance. I think he is frightfully important and considered to be very clever because of this special surgery he's so good at.'

'Oh, well, I dare say he'll come and see us one day, when he has the time.'

'Alec said that he has many friends.'

'Well, I dare say—such a handsome man and such beautiful manners. He's a man to trust, too.'

To which Margo said nothing at all. In bed later, she lay bitterly regretting what she had said to Gijs. She hadn't meant a word of it; she had been hurt and angry and had said things she really hadn't meant. She had told him that she never wanted to see him again and her heart would break if that were to happen. Never mind what he thought of her; to see him from time to time was all she asked and expected.

A week went by—a week of unpleasant November weather, cold and damp and dark but tolerated by everyone since it heralded Christmas.

Margo busied herself preparing for the forthcoming festivities—the play for the Sunday School, the making of decorations for the village hall, the wrapping of small presents for the bran tub for the children's party—and never for one moment was Gijs out of her thoughts. She did her best to banish him, to bury him beneath plans for Christmas, but that wasn't easy.

Mrs Pearson paused in her busy life from time to time and wondered what was wrong. Surely Margo wasn't regretting her decision not to marry George? When she had a few quiet moments to spare she would try to find out.

The vicar was free on Mondays and he had planned a day out, leaving Margo to mind the house and deal with any small matter which might crop up while he and her mother went to Exeter for the day. They would buy Christmas presents, treat themselves to a splendid lunch, visit the cathedral, and still have time for Mrs Pearson to indulge in some window-shopping.

Margo saw them off soon after breakfast and went back indoors to feed Caesar and Plato, clear away the dishes and get on with the housework. They would be hungry when they returned, she reflected; she would go down to the butcher and get some steak and make a casserole. It could simmer for hours on the stove and be ready when they got home.

On her return she turned the radio up, filling the

house with sound, and busied herself until lunchtime. After her meal Plato needed a walk, and by the time they were home again it was dusk and time for tea. That over, she laid the table, saw to the potatoes, made a custard to go with the plum compote she had made and sat down to wait for the sound of the car.

The six o'clock news came and went and there was on sign of them. She went to look out of the window and saw that it wasn't raining—indeed, there was a glimpse of the moon from time to time—so it wasn't the weather that was delaying them.

She picked up a book and read for a while, but when the clock struck half past seven she gave up her pretence of reading and went to the window again. Her father didn't like driving at night unless it was absolutely necessary, and he had said that they would be home before six o'clock.

'So what's happened?' Margo asked Caesar and Plato, who were sitting beside her. 'They could phone...'

The hands of the clock were creeping towards eight when there was a knock on the door, and when she went to open it Bob Passmore, the village bobby, called through the letter-box, 'It's Bob, miss, if you'll let me in.'

He was a big man with a red face and a flowing moustache, friendly with everyone. He gave the village a feeling of security—admonishing naughty boys, directing what traffic there was, cycling hither and thither on his conscientious rounds.

Now his cheerful face was serious. He came into the hall and shut the door behind him.

'Come and sit down, Miss Margo. I'm afraid I've a bit of bad news for you.'

She led the way into the sitting room. 'Mother and Father? There's been an accident?'

Bob Passmore stood in front of her. 'Yes, Miss Margo.'

'They're hurt?' She saw his face. 'They're killed?'

'I'm afraid so, Miss Margo. A car crashed into the barrier on the A303 and collided with theirs head-on. They died instantly.'

He had never known anyone so colourless and still alive.

She said quietly, 'Thank you for telling me, Bob.' She was so still that the only living thing about her was her eyes.

'You'll need to phone the family, miss. Shall I do it for you?'

'No—no, thank you, Bob. I'll ring my aunt. I'm sure she'll come here and—and help me. There will be a great deal to attend to, won't there?'

He saw that she was in shock. 'You ring your aunt while I make you a cup of tea. Would you like the wife to come over?'

'How kind of you, Bob, but I'm quite all right, and my aunt will come as soon as she can arrange it.'

'You can't be alone here, Miss Margo...'

'She'll hire a car.' She got up. 'I'll phone her now while you make the tea.'

Aunt Florence had settled down to a pleasant evening with a book from the library when the phone rang, so she lifted the receiver with a touch of impatience and said snappily, 'Hello—who is speaking?'

For a moment she didn't believe it was Margo, telling her in a voice that didn't sound like hers at all that her mother and father had been killed.

'My dear child...this is terrible. I shall come at once,

just as soon as I can get a car and pack a bag. Are you all right?'

Margo's voice telling her that she was quite all right didn't reassure her at all. So quiet and calm and without emotion.

Aunt Florence put down the phone and then picked it up again. A car—that was the first thing—and while she was waiting for it she could phone the rest of the family. She had started to dial when the doorknocker was thumped, and she went to answer it in a rush of impatience.

Someone from the village, she supposed. Well, she had no time for them now. She flung the door wide and met Professor van Kessel's smiling face.

'Oh, Professor—Gijs—how kind. Do come in. You must excuse me while I do some phoning…'

Aunt Florence, never known to lose her cool, had lost it now.

'I've had some bad news. Margo phoned not five minutes ago—her parents have been killed in a car accident. I must go to her. I'm about to arrange… You'd like a cup of coffee?'

He followed her into the sitting room. 'You want to go to Margo? I'll drive you there, Mrs Pearson. While you pack a bag I'll get you a drink; I think you need one…'

'But it's so far—I really can't impose… There's a good garage in Windsor. It can't be true—they make mistakes sometimes, don't they?'

He pushed her gently into a chair and went looking for the brandy.

'Drink this—all of it; you've had a bad shock. Tell me exactly what Margo said on the phone.'

When she had told him he said, 'Go and pack a few things while I see to doors and windows. Do you have a maid? Did I not see someone when I was here before?'

'Phoebe. She's not on the phone.'

'We will stop at her home as we go so that you can give her a key. May I use your phone?'

Aunt Florence, for once unable to cope, thankfully did as she was told. As she sat in the car some ten minutes later, it crossed her mind that he hadn't uttered one word of sympathy—but somehow that didn't matter; while others might have wasted time thinking up comforting words, he had dealt with the situation within minutes.

'Why had you come to see me?' she asked.

'I had visited Lord Trueman and I was calling to thank you for your hospitality; it was a pleasant visit.' He paused. 'Did Margo sound very upset? She was devoted to her parents, was she not?'

'Yes, she was. It didn't sound like her at all—very quiet and composed.'

'In shock. I hope that someone is with her. When she realises what has happened she will need a shoulder to cry on.'

He drove for some miles in silence, then said, 'Presumably she will have to leave the vicarage. There will be a new incumbent and he will need to live there. Has she any family other than yourself?'

'Aunts and uncles and cousins, but all but myself live in the north of England or Scotland. We are in contact—birthdays and Christmas and holidays—but I'm not sure if Margo would be happy living with any of them. Besides, she will need to find work; there won't be much money. She can come to me, of course, until she decides what she wants to do. I'm fond of her and we get on very well.'

He was driving fast, his hands relaxed on the wheel,

his face quiet. Aunt Florence wondered what he was thinking.

The journey seemed endless. 'Are we nearly there?' she asked him.

'Not long now. Try not to think about it, Mrs Pearson. I know that sounds a stupid thing to say, but Margo is going to need your help, and if you can manage to bottle up your own grief for her sake you should. It has been a terrible shock to you, I know, but I believe you to be a stout-hearted woman. Margo is a stout-hearted girl too, but the suddenness of it will have bowled her over.'

There were lights on at the vicarage as he drew up before its door. It was Bob Passmore who answered their knock.

He said in his soft Dorset voice, 'She's in the kitchen, just sitting. You'll stay? Mrs Pearson, isn't it? Her Aunt?'

Aunt Florence nodded. 'And Professor van Kessel, a friend of the family—a doctor.'

Bob Passmore looked more cheerful. 'Ah, a doctor. Maybe that'll be a help. I'll be getting along. I'll come any time you want me. There'll be more news in the morning—perhaps tonight...' He gave the professor a good look and nodded, reassured by the size of him.

Aunt Florence took off her coat and went into the kitchen, and after a moment the professor followed her.

Margo was sitting at the kitchen table with Caesar on her lap and Plato beside her. She looked up as they went in and the professor thought that she had never looked so plain; her face was quite white, with no sign of tears, but her eyes were huge.

She got slowly to her feet and Aunt Florence kissed her.

'I've come to stay, my dear, if you'll have me.'

Margo nodded. 'Thank you; that would be nice.' She looked past her to where the professor was standing.

'Gijs,' said Margo. She sounded like a frightened child. 'Oh, Gijs...'

He crossed the room and took her in his arms, holding her gently as though she were indeed a frightened child. He began to talk to her softly and suddenly she was in tears, sobbing into his shoulder, spilling out her sorrow.

He stood solid and reassuring and comforting, and after a moment Aunt Florence went to put the kettle on and gather up cups and saucers and the teapot.

Eventually Margo lifted a sodden face. 'I'm so sorry, I've soaked your jacket. I'm better now.'

He kissed her wet cheek and smiled down at her. 'That's my girl. We're going to have a cup of tea and then I'll see what I can find out for you. Then you will go to bed and sleep. In the morning it will be another day and we shall know more about everything.'

They drank their tea, not saying much, and Aunt Florence was glad to see a little colour creep back into Margo's cheeks. She studied the sad face opposite her and thanked heaven that the professor was here with them.

Presently he went away to Margo's father's study to phone, and she told Margo how it had come about that he was here with them. She talked on at random, and was relieved when he came back.

'Your mother and father are at Yeovil Hospital; it seems it was the nearest to the scene of the accident. They died instantly, Margo. There are certain formalities to be dealt with before they can be brought back here. I'll drive you there in the morning.'

'You'll stay? What about your patients? The hospital?'

'I've arranged to have a day off. I'll stay, if you'll have me.'

'Will you? Will you really?' She turned a sad face to him. 'I can't thank you enough...'

He glanced at Aunt Florence, who nodded briskly. 'An excellent idea. I'll go and make up a bed while you two get some supper. Soup, if there is any, and how about a stiff drink for all of us?'

Aunt Florence, quite restored to her usual brisk tartness, went away. She wept a little as she made up the bed and then laid out towels and soap, but she didn't give way to her grief; there would be time for that later.

Margo, comforted by Gijs's company, the sharp edge of her grief dulled for the moment, set about warming some soup while he found the plates and spoons and knives, keeping up a steady flow of talk as he did so, but making no attempt to avoid talking about her parents. Indeed, he talked about them quite cheerfully, taking no notice when she wept a little, and when she suddenly wailed, 'Oh, why did it have to happen? I don't think I can bear it...' he took her in his arms again.

'Oh, yes, you can. How would your father and mother expect you to behave? Try and think of that and take heart. My poor dear, if I could take your grief onto my shoulders I would. All I can tell you is that as each day passes the load lightens.'

Presently she swallowed her soup, took the pill he offered her and was seen into her bed by Aunt Flo. She had expected to stay awake all night, but she slept at once and only woke as a watery sun shone into her room.

She couldn't lie in bed. She got into her dressing gown and shuffled downstairs to make tea and found the professor there, standing at the open kitchen door, with Plato at his feet and Caesar tucked under one arm. He was dressed, immaculate as ever, his face calm. His good morning was friendly.

'The kettle's boiling. I was wondering if Mrs Pearson would object to me taking her a cup of tea. Now you can do it for me. Sit down; I'll make the tea. We need to leave here soon after breakfast.' He glanced at her. 'You slept?'

'Yes, thank you. I hope you were comfortable. We don't often have people staying and the bedrooms are a bit unlived-in.'

'It's a nice old house, isn't it? Built for a vicar with a large family who had to keep up appearances.'

'It's too big just for the three of us...' She faltered. 'It *was* too big, I mean.' She drank some tea. 'Of course I shall have to go, won't I?'

'Yes. Although I should imagine they will give you a little time. You will go to your aunt?'

'I expect so, if she doesn't mind. Just while I find some work somewhere.' She finished her tea. 'I'll take her a cup. Will breakfast in about half an hour be all right?'

The formalities, once they reached Yeovil, seemed endless to her. The professor had suggested that he should identify her mother and father for her and she had nodded wordlessly, and afterwards he had said, 'They both look peaceful and there is no sign of injury. Would you like me to arrange their return to Thinbottom?'

He had done that, and attended to all the other arrangements which had to be made, and then driven her back home to find Aunt Florence waiting for them with a substantial tea.

'I have telephoned the rest of the family,' she told Margo, 'and there have been a great many telephone calls for you. I've left a list on your father's desk. You will be kept busy for a while, Margo. Will it be a good idea if I see to the cooking and the house, so that you are free to see people and write the letters and answer the phone?'

The professor took Plato for a walk while they washed up the tea things, and when he returned observed that he would have to return to London that evening.

'I'll come to the funeral if I may,' he said. 'I dare say you'll know more about the future in a few days' time.'

Margo summed up a smile. 'Yes, of course. You've been so kind—I can never repay you.'

She had made a great effort to behave normally in his company. He had been kind and dealt with everything without fuss. Now she wished him goodbye in a determinedly cheerful voice, offering a hand and wishing with all her heart that his large, comforting one would never let it go.

It was Aunt Florence, bustling into the hall, who made it unnecessary for her to say anything more.

'Margo, there's someone—a Reverend Mac-something—on the phone. Would you speak to him?'

When Margo had gone she said, 'Margo will have thanked you; now it's my turn. I don't know how we could have managed without you. Bless you, Gijs.' She put out her hand. 'Do you think that is the new incumbent already? Surely not...' Her severe features crumpled. 'What is to happen to Margo?'

The professor held her hand and bent and kissed her cheek.

'Why, I shall marry her,' he said, in a no-nonsense voice.

He didn't give her time to reply to that but got into his car. It was out of sight when Margo came back into the hall.

CHAPTER FIVE

FOR Margo, the next few days were like a bad dream; she walked and talked, signed forms, answered letters and listened politely to endless sympathy and some good advice, but it seemed to her that it was another person doing these things, a calm, quiet girl, who washed and dressed herself and ate her meals like an automaton. Presently, she told herself repeatedly, she would wake up from the nightmare.

All the while she was scarcely aware of the professor, dealing with the whole unhappy business, sparing her as much as he could with silent efficiency.

It was Aunt Florence who asked him worriedly if he was getting enough rest, for he drove back and forth, fitting in his visits with his hospital work, his ward rounds, his clinics, theatre lists and private patients.

She had to be content with his quiet assurance that he was perfectly all right, but the tired lines on his weary face disquieted her.

'It is only for a few days more,' he reminded her, smiling.

It was after the funeral, when everyone had left the vicarage and the three of them were standing in the sitting room surrounded by the debris of cups and saucers and plates and left-over food, that he said briskly to Margo, 'We're going for a walk while Mrs Pearson puts her feet up for an hour. Go and get a coat, Margo.'

It was a bright, cold day, the sun already low, but there was still an hour or more of daylight. They set off along the road out of the village, not talking, comfortable in each other's company, with Plato plodding happily beside them. They had walked for half an hour when the professor said, 'This is where we met, Margo,' and stood still and wrapped his arms around her. Great comforting arms, whose warmth after all these days allowed her to give way to her sorrow.

She sobbed and snivelled, mumbling into his shoulder until there were no more tears left. When at last she raised her head, he said cheerfully, 'That's better,' and mopped her face with his handkerchief.

'So sorry,' said Margo on a last hiccup. 'It was all bottled up inside me. I feel better now.'

'You will go on feeling better and better each day. If you want to cry, then do so, Margo. You don't have to be brave with me.'

She couldn't see his face clearly in the gathering dusk. 'You have been very kind. I don't know what I should have done without you...'

'I hope that there will be no need to be without me. Will you marry me, Margo?'

She lifted a tear-stained face to his and peered at him. 'Marry you? You mean us—marry? But we don't—you don't know me; I might not suit you at all. I can't think of any reason...'

'Two very good ones. I need a wife and you need a home. What is more, I believe that we shall get along very well together. In other circumstances I would have suggested that we had the usual engagement and got to know each other, but, as things are, it seems to me that we should marry first and get to know each other afterwards.'

He had turned her round and was walking her back the way they had come.

'You're not hankering after George?'

She answered with some of her usual spirit. 'Good heavens, no. What about you, though?'

'Am I hankering? No. I'm thirty-five, Margo. I've been in and out of love a dozen times. Now I want to settle down, and I should like to do that with you.'

She stopped walking and tugged at his arm. 'It wouldn't work even if I said yes. I have no looks, and it's no use pretending that I have, and I've no idea how the wife of a famous surgeon should behave.' She paused. 'Besides, you're Dutch.'

'So I am,' he said mildly. 'But I'm still Gijs.' He took hold of the hand on his sleeve and held it fast. 'I imagine surgeons' wives behave exactly the same way as any other wife would. And one thing more—you have beautiful eyes, Margo; nothing else matters.'

They walked on in silence until Margo said in a small voice, 'Thank you for asking me, Gijs. I think I'd like to marry you. Not because I need a home, but because I do like you. Only there's a condition. You must promise to tell me if ever you should fall in love…'

'I promise—but you must promise too.'

As a vicar's daughter, she had been brought up not to tell lies. But surely this particular lie wouldn't count as much? 'I promise,' said Margo.

He tucked her hand back into his arm. 'You will be staying here for a few more days, to pack up before the new vicar arrives? Aunt Florence will be with you? Good. I'll come again as soon as I can. Shall we marry as soon as possible? I intend to go over to Holland three days before Christmas. We could marry in the morning and travel on the same day. A quiet wedding?'

'Yes, please. Just us. Well, Aunt Florence will want to be there.' She asked hesitantly, 'Do you have any family, Gijs?'

'My mother died ten years ago; my father died last

year. I have three sisters and a brother. Since we shall be going to Holland directly after the wedding you can meet them all then. Would you like to be married here?'

She said, 'Yes, please,' and swallowed sudden tears. 'I expect Sir William would give me away.'

'That's settled, then.' They had reached the vicarage and went in through the kitchen. Aunt Florence came marching through the door as they went in.

'Splendid—just in time to help with the washing-up. Gijs, you'll stay for supper? I'll get it ready now; you'll want to get back.'

'Aunt Flo, Gijs has asked me to marry him and I said I would.'

Her aunt's severe features broke into a smile. 'That is splendid news. When is the wedding to be?'

She embraced Margo and looked at Gijs.

'We intend to marry three days before Christmas and go over to Holland on the same day.' He nodded, took off his overcoat and jacket and rolled up his shirt-sleeves. 'I'll wash,' he told Margo, 'and you wipe.'

He went after supper, kissing Aunt Florence's cheek and then Margo's. His kiss was swift, and not in the least lover-like. Margo hadn't expected that anyway.

When he had driven away, Margo asked anxiously, 'I'm doing the right thing, aren't I, Aunt Flo? I'm not marrying him for a home, although I know I need one, and I do like him very much...'

Aunt Flo said something which sounded like 'pish' and 'tosh'. 'My dear child, you're marrying him because you love him, aren't you? So of course you are doing the right thing.'

Margo was horrified. 'How did you know? I never said a word...'

'Don't worry, he hasn't noticed—nor will he unless you want him to.'

She gave Margo a brisk pat on the shoulder. 'Now, we are going to occupy ourselves this evening with plans for your wedding—something your mother and father would have wanted you to do. Get some paper and a pen, child, and let us begin.'

The evening, which Margo had been dreading, went quickly. There wasn't much money but, as Aunt Flo pointed out, there was only need to buy suitable clothes for her wedding and the time she would spend in Holland.

'I imagine Gijs will want to see you suitably dressed. You will be able to fit yourself out when you return after Christmas, but you must have some new clothes before then.'

Margo's list was short, but she insisted that it was adequate. 'If I could find a dress and jacket for the wedding, then I could wear the dress later. My winter coat's still good enough. I'll get a jersey two-piece. And a tweed skirt perhaps? I've several blouses and woollies. Something for the evening?'

'Most certainly.'

'A skirt? Velvet, I think.' Margo wrote busily. 'One of those cream crêpe blouses with a waterfall collar, and another blouse or top…'

'Shoes?' Aunt Florence reminded her. 'And gloves and a decent handbag—very important.'

She glanced at the clock and saw with satisfaction that the evening which they had both secretly dreaded had reached a time when she could reasonably suggest a hot drink and bed.

'Tomorrow,' said Aunt Flo, 'we will go through your clothes and make them ready. I've no doubt there will be buttons to sew on and so forth.'

So presently they went to their beds, each assuring the other that they were very tired and would sleep at once.

Neither of them did, but that was neither here nor there.

A bright, cold morning cheered their spirits. They met for breakfast with determined cheerfulness, discussing the weather at some length, reading the letters of condolence which were still coming and debating what they would have for their lunch. They were weighing the advantages of poached eggs on spinach against toasted cheese when the phone rang.

'Margo?' The professor's voice was reassuringly placid. 'I expect you want to do some shopping? If I come for you both tomorrow morning at about nine o'clock, could you be ready? I'll drive you back around six o'clock. I'll have to work until then.'

'Oh, yes, please. But that makes an awfully long day for you, Gijs. Whatever time will you have to leave London to get to us by nine o'clock? Would you like breakfast?'

'No, no. It's no great distance, you know, and I enjoy driving. Only be ready for me, won't you? I'll see you then.'

He rang off before she could say anything else, and her goodbye fell on silence. She told herself that he was probably busy.

Which he was—going to scrub for a morning's surgery in Theatre, with Margo, for the moment, dismissed from his mind.

With the shopping to look forward to the day went quickly. Margo went down to the village and arranged with Mrs Twigg, who had come to the vicarage for years to do the rough work once a week, to spend the day there and look after Caesar and Plato and at the same time do some cleaning.

'Going out for the day?' she wanted to know. 'Do you good, Miss Margo, what with one thing and another.'

'Yes, my aunt and I are going to London. Professor van Kessel is coming for us...'

'Ah, yes, 'im as is sweet on you, Miss Margo.'

Margo blushed. 'Well, no, not exactly, Mrs Twigg. That is, we're going to be married. Very quietly and soon.'

'Lor' bless you, miss, that's the best bit of news I've heard for quite a while. You deserve to be happy, and he looks a nice kind of gentleman.'

'Yes, he is!' said Margo. 'We haven't told anyone yet...'

When the paper arrived later, Aunt Florence was quick to point out the announcement of their engagement. Since most of the vicar's friends and the parishioners took that same paper, the phone didn't stop ringing all the morning.

The professor, leaving London very early the next morning, had a good deal to think about. He had dealt with the special licence, arranged his work at the hospital, conferred with his secretary concerning his private patients and discussed his theatre lists with Theatre Sister. There was also the question of finding a house in London, buying it and furnishing it—in the meantime they would have to rent a flat. His secretary, a highly efficient middle-aged lady, had already procured any number of leaflets on suitable houses, and as soon as he could spare the time he would go and look at the best of them. Then there was Holland. He hoped Margo would like his home, since it was going to be her home too.

They were waiting for him, with Mrs Twigg peering from the kitchen, anxious not to miss a moment. He kissed Aunt Florence's cheek, kissed Margo's too, bent to pat Plato, complimented them on their punctuality and ushered them into the car.

Margo, he reflected, looked better. There was colour in her cheeks and her eyes shone—with the expectancy of a day's outing, he supposed. Her hat, he decided, was unbecoming—bought to last, as a mere covering for the head with no pretensions to fashion. It would be interesting to see what the right clothes would do for her when they were married.

To make up for his thoughts, he gave her a warm smile as he started the car.

They didn't talk much as they went. Margo sensed that he needed to get back as quickly as possible, and indeed he drove fast. The road was comparatively empty until they reached the outskirts of London, and even there the early morning rush-hour was over and there were no major hold-ups.

He set them down at Marble Arch. 'Take a taxi to the hospital—be there by six o'clock and wait for me in the reception hall. Have a good day!'

He opened her door and got out to help Aunt Florence.

'Have you enough money?'

'Yes, thank you, Gijs. We'll see you at six o'clock.'

They watched the Rolls slip back into the traffic. 'What a thoughtful man he is,' said Aunt Flo, and took Margo's arm. 'Let's find a place for coffee and then get down to the shopping.'

It wasn't too difficult to find a skirt and woollies, and Margo soon found the evening skirt she wanted. She found the blouse too, and a rather more elaborate top in a delicate apricot. They stopped for a sandwich and then began to hunt for the dress and jacket.

They found it at last in a boutique in Regent Street—just the shade of blue Margo had wished for—and, urged by the sales lady, she bought a hat to go with it. A small velvet affair which perched charmingly on her pale brown hair.

Aunt Flo, not to be outdone, bought her slippers for the evening—black satin with dainty heels. 'You'll both get a wedding present when you get back to London,' she said gruffly. 'And now I could do with a cup of tea.'

After their tea, mindful of the rush-hour, they hailed a taxi to take them to the hospital, where the head porter ushered them to seats against the wall, away from the constant flow of people going in and out.

They sat for some time, surrounded by their parcels and packages, until Margo, incurably inquisitive, got to her feet and wandered off with the whisper that she was only going to look down the various corridors which had aroused her curiosity.

The first one ended in a staircase she didn't quite dare to go up, so she retraced her steps, saw that Aunt Florence was still sitting there alone, and tried the next. This was much more promising, with doors on either side and leading to another even wider corridor. She peered round a corner and looked straight at the professor, standing with two other men only yards from her. He looked quite different in his long white coat, with a pile of papers under one arm: remote and a stranger.

He was looking directly at her; his faint smile was barely perceptible and his slight shake of the head allowed her to release a held breath as she melted back round the corner and sped back to Aunt Flo.

'And what did you find?'

'Well, Gijs is at the end of that corridor, talking to two men. He saw me.' Margo sounded a little doubtful.

'Annoyed, was he?'

'I don't think so. I'm not sure.'

'Well, here he comes, so you'll soon know,' said Aunt Flo briskly.

Beyond apologising for keeping them waiting, he had nothing more to say—only enquired about their day's shopping and ushered them out into the forecourt and into the Rolls.

Presently, sitting beside him as he drove through the city, Margo asked, 'Are you annoyed with me? I wasn't snooping around looking for you; I just wanted to see where the corridor went.'

'I'm disappointed—I'd hoped you *were* looking for me—and of course I'm not annoyed. Don't be a silly goose!'

Reassuring, perhaps, but she wasn't sure if he was joking. She rather thought that he was. She must take care not to encroach on his work and to leave him alone until, hopefully, they settled down together.

Mrs Twigg had not only dusted and polished, she had also cooked supper, and had it waiting for them when they arrived.

'One of my steak and kidney pies,' she told Margo, tucking her wages into a shabby purse, 'and an apple crumble to follow. Had a good day's shopping, have you, Miss Margo?'

'Lovely, Mrs Twigg. I got all I needed to buy.'

She was conscious of Gijs standing at her elbow, and then Mrs Twigg said cheerfully, 'Well, she'll make a pretty little bride, I'm sure, sir.'

'Indeed she will, Mrs Twigg. I'll take you home if you're ready.'

'Lor', sir, that's not necessary. It's but ten minutes' walk...'

'Two minutes in the car.'

He was longer than two minutes. Margo took off her outdoor things, laid the table and cast an eye into the oven while Aunt Florence sat by the sitting-room fire. With just one table-lamp on and the firelight the room didn't look too bad.

Margo, poking her head round the door, said, 'When Gijs gets back I'll see if there's any sherry left...'

He came in a few minutes later, a bottle under his arm.

'Mrs Twigg's pie smells delicious,' he said, and strolled into the kitchen to look for a corkscrew to open the bottle.

Margo, poking the sprouts to see if they were cooked, turned to look. 'Champagne...'

'We have all had a hard day. Where are the glasses, Margo?'

Supper was a cheerful meal; there was plenty to talk about and it was getting late when Gijs got up to go. Margo, about to worry aloud about the brief night's sleep ahead of him, bit the words back, told him mildly to drive carefully and thanked him for taking them to London. 'It was a really lovely day.' She smiled brightly, but he saw the sadness in her eyes.

'I'm going to be busy for a few days. When do you leave here?'

'In two days' time. I sold the car to the garage, but Jim Potts, who owns it, will drive us and the animals and luggage.'

He nodded. 'Splendid—otherwise I would have arranged a car...'

'Thank you for thinking of it,' she told him gravely, 'but everyone in the village has been so kind. I've had so much help.'

He smiled at her and bent to kiss her cheek. 'Don't be too sad, Margo; we will make a happy life together.' He took her hand. 'Ah—I had almost forgotten.'

He searched around in a pocket and took out a small plush case and opened it. There was a ring inside—a splendid sapphire surrounded by diamonds.

'It is old and has been in the family for many years. I hope it fits—my mother had small hands very like yours.'

She held out her hand and he slipped it onto her finger.

'Oh, it's so beautiful,' said Margo. 'And it fits exactly. I hope your mother would have liked me to have it.' She reached up and kissed his cheek. 'Thank you, Gijs; I'm very proud to wear it.'

He touched her cheek with a gentle finger. 'I'll phone,' he told her, 'and see you again as soon as possible. I have a backlog of work to deal with.'

'I understand. You've already done too much for me. Please forget me until the wedding. I'm quite all right, really I am.' She added matter-of-factly, 'I don't intend to interfere with your work; I know it's important to you. Mother never stood in Father's way when it came to his parish work, and I won't stand in yours.'

He looked down at her earnest face and suddenly smiled. 'I believe I have found a treasure,' he told her, and the next minute he was gone.

Margo, busy with her final packing and goodbyes and then transporting herself, her aunt and the animals and luggage to Sunningfield, none the less wondered from time to time if Gijs would phone. She had told him not

PLAY...

"ROLL A DOUBLE!"

GET 2 BOOKS
AND A
FABULOUS MYSTERY BONUS GIFT

ABSOLUTELY FREE!

SEE INSIDE...

(U-H-R-11/98) 116 HDL CJQ9

NO RISK, NO OBLIGATION TO BUY...NOW OR EVER!

GUARANTEED

PLAY "ROLL A DOUBLE" AND YOU GET FREE GIFTS! HERE'S HOW TO PLAY:

1. Peel off label from front cover. Place it in space provided at right. With a coin, carefully scratch off the silver dice. Then check the claim chart to see what we have for you – TWO FREE BOOKS and a mystery gift – ALL YOURS! ALL FREE!

2. Send back this card and you'll receive brand-new Harlequin Romance® novels. These books have a cover price of $3.50 each, but they are yours to keep absolutely free.

3. There's no catch. You're under no obligation to buy anything. We charge nothing – ZERO – for your first shipment. And you don't have to make any minimum number of purchases – not even one!

4. The fact is, thousands of readers enjoy receiving books by mail from the Harlequin Reader Service®. They like the convenience of home delivery...they like getting the best new novels BEFORE they're available in stores...and they love our discount prices!

5. We hope that after receiving your free books you'll want to remain a subscriber. But the choice is yours – to continue or cancel any time at all! So why not take us up on our invitation, with no risk of any kind. You'll be glad you did!

*THIS MYSTERY BONUS GIFT COULD BE YOURS **FREE** WHEN YOU PLAY "ROLL A DOUBLE"*

"ROLL A DOUBLE!"

Place label here

SCRATCH HERE

SEE CLAIM CHART BELOW

116 HDL CJQ9
(U-H-R-11/98)

YES! I have placed my label from the front cover into the space provided above and scratched off the silver dice. Please send me all the gifts for which I qualify. I understand that I am under no obligation to purchase any books, as explained on the back and on the opposite page.

Name

(PLEASE PRINT)

Address _____ Apt.#

City _____ State _____ Zip

CLAIM CHART

🎲🎲	**2 FREE BOOKS PLUS MYSTERY BONUS GIFT**
🎲🎲	**2 FREE BOOKS**
🎲🎲	**1 FREE BOOK**

CLAIM NO.37-829

All orders subject to approval. Offer limited to one per household.

The Harlequin Reader Service®— Here's how it works:

Accepting free books places you under no obligation to buy anything. You may keep the books and gift and return the shipping statement marked "cancel." If you do not cancel, about a month later we'll send you 6 additional novels and bill you just $2.90 each, plus 25¢ delivery per book and applicable sales tax, if any.* That's the complete price — and compared to cover prices of $3.50 each — quite a bargain! You may cancel at any time, but if you choose to continue, every month we'll send you 6 more books, which you may either purchase at the discount price...or return to us and cancel your subscription.

*Terms and prices subject to change without notice. Sales tax applicable in N.Y.

to worry about her, but surely, she reflected, it would take only a few minutes to ring up. He couldn't be working all day—and what about the evenings?

The professor was doing just that: working a long day, seeing his private patients in the evenings and catching up on the paperwork before he went to bed. He hadn't forgotten Margo, but he had tidied her away to the back of his mind for the time being—although he *had* found time to arrange to rent a small house in a quiet street close to Wimpole Street, where he had his consulting rooms. It was furnished and had a tiny walled garden; it would serve its purpose until they had a house of their own.

Late one evening he phoned his home in Holland and, well satisfied with the result, took himself off to bed…

As for Margo, she saw to a bewildered Plato and Caesar, unpacked her few clothes and set to with a will to put Aunt Flo's house to rights again. She also opened the various parcels she had been given from well-wishers in the village.

Sir William and Lady Frost had given her a charming painting of flowers, several people in the village had clubbed together and given her a cut-glass fruit bowl, and George and his mother had sent a pair of book-ends—bronze pigs, which somehow seemed suitable since George bred them.

Lord and Lady Trueman sent over a splendid porcelain vase, and Helen a charming small silver clock, and by the morning's post there came a shower of gifts from friends and relatives.

Margo begged a large, stout box from the village shop and packed everything away and then sat down to write thank-you letters. It was a pity Gijs wasn't there to see their gifts; she supposed that they would help to furnish wherever they were going to live.

The thought brought her up short; it was something she hadn't really thought about. Would they live in London or Holland or both? Perhaps they would make their home in Holland and Gijs would travel to and fro, just as he did now? Where would they go to live when they came back after Christmas? Unless he planned to leave her there. The idea was a bit daunting...

It was two days after she had moved to her aunt's when he phoned, quite late in the evening.

'I shall be free tomorrow after midday—may I fetch you to spend the rest of the day with me in town? There are several things to see to... Is everything all right? You've settled in with Aunt Florence?'

'I'm fine; we both are. What time will you come?'

'Some time after twelve o'clock. We'll talk then.'

She heard him speaking to someone, and then he said, 'I have to go, Margo. Tomorrow.'

When she told her aunt, that lady said, 'What will you wear?'

'My winter coat and the jersey dress. I don't suppose we'll go anywhere very fashionable, do you?'

The next morning was clear and cold; Margo got into the jersey dress, found her good gloves and shoes and handbag, and did her hair with more care than usual. Even so her sensible hat didn't look anything other than dowdy, but it was far too cold to go without anything on her head. She hoped that Gijs wouldn't notice...

He did, of course, but it didn't matter. He greeted her with a kiss, spent five minutes asking after Aunt Florence's health, then popped Margo into the car and drove back to London.

'Why do you want me to come with you?' asked Margo, never one to mince her words.

'We have to buy the wedding rings. Let us do that first.'

He took her to Garrard's, where, in the quiet surroundings, she chose a plain gold ring for herself and then, at his smiling nod, one for him. She hoped that they didn't cost too much, for no price was mentioned; presumably Gijs was satisfied, as he got out his chequebook. She wandered away to look at the magnificent jewels on display, and was contemplating a brooch—a true lover's knot in diamonds—when he joined her.

He asked casually if she liked it. 'Well, of course I do—it's magnificent. But I wouldn't want it...'

'Why not?'

'Me and diamonds don't go together,' said Margo ungrammatically. 'They don't, do they? Be honest.'

She felt unreasonably disappointed when he agreed with her.

She was a sensible girl; she had asked for an honest answer and she had got it, and in a way she was glad that he liked her enough not to pretend to something he didn't feel. She smiled up at him. 'Thank you for my ring. What do you want to do next?'

'Coffee while I tell you.'

He turned down a side-street and ushered her into a small café. When the coffee came he told her about the house. 'I hope you will like it,' he finished. 'It is the best that I can do at short notice. We'll go there next, and after we've had lunch we will go and look at houses...'

'Houses?' echoed Margo. 'But haven't we got one? You just said...'

'Well, we have to have a home of sorts until we get

one of our own. The agent has several lined up for us to look at.'

'You mean to buy a house?'

'I come over to England several times a year; we shall need a home to come to.' He smiled at her. 'Am I rushing you along too fast? Shall we go? The meter will have almost run out.'

He drove with no sign of impatience through the heavy traffic, and then they were in comparative quiet.

'Wimpole Street,' said Margo, looking out of the window. 'Don't doctors have their rooms here?'

'Yes, and Harley Street. If you look on the right you'll see a green-painted door with a brass plate beside it. I've my rooms there. The house I have rented is down this side-street.'

Margo found it quite perfect. It had a glossy black-painted door, with tubs on either side, and inside there was a narrow hall with a sitting room on one side and a dining room on the other, both furnished comfortably. The kitchen was modern and small, there was a tiny cloakroom under the circular stairs, and a door leading to the garden and another small room, which she supposed Gijs would use as a study.

Two bedrooms faced the street, with a bathroom between them, and a third room overlooked the garden. There was a short passage with a door on one side of it, opening onto a quite large room furnished as a bed-sitting-room, with an alcove holding a shower and a large window.

'The housekeeper's room,' said Gijs, consulting the leaflet in his hand.

'Well, I suppose so—but we don't need one, do we? I'm quite a good cook and it's a very small house.'

'We shall need someone in to do the cleaning. Would

you be happy here for a short time while we find our own home?'

'Oh, yes. It's delightful and very quiet. Can we come straight here when we come back from Holland?'

'Yes. I've the keys already.' He led the way downstairs and out to the car. 'When we have had lunch we will take a look at the houses I thought might suit us. I've arranged to meet the agent.'

He took her to the Ritz, and Margo prudently left her coat and the regrettable hat in the cloakroom. Her clothes were all wrong, but since Gijs didn't seem to mind she decided that she wouldn't either. She looked around her at the magnificent room as they sat down at a table overlooking the gardens.

'It's truly splendid, isn't it?' she observed. 'Just being here without eating would be a treat...'

He laughed. 'I know what you mean, but I for one am hungry.'

So was Margo. She ate Galia melon, Dover sole with Dauphin potatoes and braised chicory and, while Gijs pondered the cheeseboard, she chose orange crème soufflé.

Over coffee, she asked, 'Do you have a lot of friends in England, Gijs?'

'Yes. Most of them people I work with. There are several Dutch friends living over here too. You will meet them all, of course. Gijs van der Eekerk and his wife Beatrice have a flat near Green Park, but, just as I do, he goes back to Holland from time to time.' He put down his coffee-cup. 'Shall we go and see what the estate agent has lined up for us?'

He was waiting for them at the first house, a handsome Georgian residence, one of a row lining a quiet street close to Cavendish Square. 'Opulent' was the only way to describe it, reflected Margo, and it wasn't even furnished. Asked if she liked it, she firmly said no. She said no to the second house too, a three-story Regency house with a semi-basement. The third house she fell in love with instantly. Just as Gijs had hoped she would.

It was at the end of a row of mews cottages, and it was as delightful inside as out. A good deal larger than she'd expected, too, with a long, low room on one side of the door, two smaller rooms on the other side of the hall, and a good-sized kitchen at the back, beside which was a pleasant room with its own shower room.

Upstairs—reached by a graceful little staircase—there were three bedrooms, another shower room and a large bathroom, and through a door at the back of the landing was a short staircase leading to a large attic.

The professor, leaning against a door, watching her, asked, 'Do you like it, Margo?'

'Yes, oh, yes, I do. It's...' She paused to think. 'It's like a home,' she finished lamely. 'Do you like it?'

'Yes, I do.' He smiled and crossed the room to stand in front of her. 'Shall we buy it?'

'Oh, could we? It won't be too expensive? This is rather a splendid part of London, isn't it?'

'It's so convenient for my rooms,' he reminded her. 'About ten minutes' walk. Hyde Park and Green Park are both within easy walking distance; so are Bond Street and Regent Street. I think it will suit us both admirably.'

'There's a tiny garden at the back,' she told him. 'But what about a garage?'

'Being the last in the row, we have a double one at the side.' He took her hand in his. 'You're sure?'

When she nodded, he said, 'Then let us go to the agent's office and settle the matter.'

As they went back downstairs he observed, 'The

place has been put in good order. I'll have to have it surveyed, of course, but by the time we come back from Holland it should be ours and you can set about furnishing it.'

'You too—it's your home as well.'

'A pleasant thought,' he said, and smiled at her again.

The agent's office was palatial, in a quiet street somewhere behind Harrods. She had had no idea that buying a house was so easy. She supposed that there would be no mortgage; it seemed to her the kind of place where one handed over a cheque with the minimum of fuss. Which was just what the professor was doing. If she had known the size of the deposit he was paying, let alone the price of the house, strong girl though she was, she would probably have fainted.

As it was, she speculated about Gijs's income. It must be a good one, of course; he drove a Rolls-Royce, didn't he? And his shoes were hand-made, his clothes discreetly elegant. She supposed she would get used to his lifestyle in time, but she had never been a girl to hanker after things she knew she could never have. It would be nice to be able to have some fashionable clothes...

The business dealt with, they went in search of tea. He took her to Brown's Hotel where, she saw at once, he was known, and enjoyed a delicious tea—tiny sandwiches, mouth-watering cakes, and muffins in a covered dish. Drinking Earl Grey tea, she remembered the strong brew offered in a mug which he had drunk with every evidence of enjoyment at the vicarage.

He drove her back to Sunningfield then, but he didn't stay for long. She hid her disappointment behind a bright smile and thanked him for her day, laughingly agreeing that the next time they saw each other it would be on their wedding day.

Seeing him off from Aunt Flo's door, she speculated as to how he would be spending his evening. He had been in a carefully concealed hurry to go back to London. Perhaps he was dining with friends, or just one friend—a woman, perhaps. A final fling before he married.

Margo allowed her imagination to run riot; only Aunt Flo's voice begging her to come in and shut the door brought her back to good sense again. Gijs, she told herself firmly, was entitled to do what he wanted without her poking her nose into his affairs. She joined her aunt in the sitting room and gave her a detailed account of her day.

She thought about him again, though, once she was in bed.

It was a pity for her peace of mind that she didn't know that the professor had driven straight to the hospital; there was a very ill child there, not yet diagnosed, and he had said that he would return that evening and do more tests. He remained at the hospital for some hours, forgetful of dinner, of the house he had just bought, and even forgetful—just for the time being—of Margo.

CHAPTER SIX

THE days until the wedding flashed by in a dream. Sometimes Margo woke in the night convinced that she was making a dreadful mistake, that she must have been out of her mind to agree to marry Gijs. In the small hours the future loomed, fraught with pitfalls: his family, his friends—and he had many, he had told her— the prospect of entertaining them, of buying the right clothes, and that lovely little house which he expected her to furnish. She would fall asleep again eventually, and when she woke it would be morning and all that mattered was that she loved him...

They were to be married at eleven o'clock. Gijs came to fetch them just before nine o'clock.

'This is most unorthodox,' observed Aunt Florence, majestic in a new hat. 'The bridegroom should never see his bride before she comes to him in church.'

'In Holland,' the professor told her placidly, 'the bridegroom goes to fetch his bride with a bouquet and they go to be married together. Where is Margo?'

'I'm here.' She came quietly downstairs, feeling shy, anxious that he should like her outfit.

He crossed the small hall and bent to kiss her. 'What a charming outfit, and I do like the hat.'

She smiled up at him, reflecting sadly that he might have been a brother or a cousin, even an old friend from his manner—certainly not a man in love. Sitting beside him in the Rolls presently, she reminded herself that he wasn't in love with anyone, so why shouldn't he fall in love with her? First she must attract his attention—the right clothes, an elegant house, entertaining his friends, a good hairdresser and the discreet application of the beauty aids recommended in the glossy magazines. All this must be done slowly; first she must get to know his family and something of his life. It would probably take years, she reflected, but it would be worth it.

Gijs kept up a flow of small talk as he drove, with Aunt Florence chipping in from time to time, but presently he said, 'You're very quiet, Margo—cold feet?'

'No.' She turned to smile at him. 'What about you?'

'Certainly not. I have always understood that bridegrooms dread getting married—dozens of guests, satin and wedding veil, bridesmaids, wedding cakes and getting showered with confetti—but since none of these will bother us I'm looking forward to being married.'

'When I married your uncle,' said Aunt Flo from the back seat, 'he shook like a leaf throughout the service and he trod on my train.'

At the church, Gijs parked the car, handed Margo over to Sir William and went with Aunt Flo. Two minutes later they followed them, and as the church door was opened Margo was surprised to hear the organ. It would be old Miss Twittchitt playing: Margo could hear the wrong notes. She had played for years and no one would have dreamt of suggesting a successor. The verger was just inside the door, beaming at her, handing her a small bouquet as Sir William began to march down the aisle, sweeping her along with him.

The church was full; every single person from the village was there, smiling and nodding as they went. She clutched Sir William's sleeve and he patted her hand.

'A surprise, eh? Well, we've all known you for years, my dear.'

She glanced at Gijs when she reached his side and he half smiled at her. She wanted to ask him if he had known about it, but knew it would hardly do with the new vicar standing by waiting to marry them.

He began the service and she gave him her full attention. Only when it was time for the ring to be placed on her finger did she realise that there was a man standing beside Gijs. A big man, about Gijs's age, perhaps older, who handed over the ring without a fuss, smiling a little.

Presently, as they stood at the church door while people took photos, she asked who he was.

'Gijs van der Eekerk. Beatrice is here too; you'll meet her soon.' He took her arm. 'Come along; Sir William and his wife have laid on a reception—the entire village will be there.'

'Oh—did you know?'

'Yes. He rang me a couple of days ago, but I thought it would be best to surprise you.' He smiled. 'It isn't quite the wedding we planned, is it? But they all love you, Margo.'

Margo, cutting the wedding cake with Gijs's firm, cool hand over hers, said quietly, 'Won't we miss the ferry?'

'We're going on a later one. We shall get home for supper instead of tea.'

She met Beatrice and Gijs van der Eekerk; she liked them both and it was nice to think that she would see more of them in London as well as in Holland—it somehow made the future more solid. She and Gijs went from one group to the next in the Frosts' vast drawing room, bidding people goodbye, exchanging plans to meet again at some time and finally thanking Sir William for their reception.

He beamed at them. 'Well, what I mean to say is, Lady Frost said to me, "William, I insist on having Margo here with her husband. The village is sorry to see her go." She is quite right too. Hope you'll be very happy and all that.'

Aunt Florence, buoyed up by champagne, wished them a safe journey. 'I know you'll be happy,' she told them. 'Come and see me when you get back. I'll look after Caesar and Plato.'

Her sharp nose, slightly pinkened by champagne, quivered. 'I shall miss you both.'

Margo hugged her. 'Of course we'll come and see you when we get back. Have a happy Christmas with Lord Trueman's family.'

Guests surged around them, showering them with confetti and shouting their good wishes as they drove away.

'Comfortable?' asked Gijs. 'I don't want to stop on the way unless we have to. I'm going to Southampton then onto the M3 and up to the ring road at Reigate. Dull driving, but fast. I've booked us on the seven o'clock hovercraft from Dover.'

There wasn't much traffic until they reached the M25; he had kept up his speed and even with the congested motorway here he slid effortlessly ahead. Margo sat quietly, content to watch his hands, which were relaxed on the wheel, exchanging the odd remark with him from time to time and reminding herself that she was married, that they were on their way to Holland and the future was an unopened book for her.

The wedding had been an unforgettable occasion. She thought wistfully that her mother and father would have enjoyed every minute of it—a happy finish to her old life. The new, she promised herself, would be happy too; she had so much and she loved Gijs—never mind if he felt only a mild affection for her.

It was dark by the time they reached Dover, and they were among the last of the passengers to go on board. Margo, glad to be out of the car for a while, assured Gijs that she saw no reason to feel seasick, accepted the coffee she was offered and looked around her.

There was plenty to see and Gijs, secretly amused at her interest, found himself enjoying her unselfconscious pleasure and laying himself out to entertain her. Once they had landed he took care to point out their route, finding a revived interest in a journey which he made so frequently that he usually scarcely noticed the country through which he drove. They would drive along the coast to Ostend, where he would turn off to Ghent, take the motorway to Antwerp, bypass that city and so go on to Breda.

They had had tea on board and he had told her then that there was a fairly long journey before them. 'If you want to stop, you must just say so, Margo,' he said now. 'For we have all the time in the world.'

'Just how far is it? Where are we going...?'

'A few miles the other side of Utrecht. Less than an hour's drive once we reach Breda. Breda is roughly a hundred and thirty miles from here.' He glanced at his watch. 'It's half past eight; we should be home in three hours—probably less.'

Probably less, reflected Margo as the Rolls raced along roads which Gijs evidently knew well. He was a splendid driver, and on a road frequently empty of traffic he gave the Rolls her head.

Presently Margo said, 'Don't think I'm criticising— I like going fast—but is there a speed limit in Belgium?'

He laughed. 'Yes, but it's largely ignored. You like driving?'

'Yes, very much.'

'We must get you a car. There's not much point in having one in London, but here we live in the country—close enough to Utrecht and Amsterdam, but I shall be away all day and you'll want to be independent.'

Margo agreed. She had no wish to be independent—she would like to stick to him like a leech—but that was a thought she prudently kept to herself.

She had plenty to think about and she guessed that Gijs would dislike it if she chattered. Besides, she wasn't much good at small talk. She mused over their day and then allowed her thoughts to dwell on her life at Thinbottom. They were sad thoughts; her grief for her parents was still something she hadn't quite come to terms with.

When Gijs said suddenly, 'Are you thinking about Thinbottom and your parents?' she gave a gasp.

'How did you know? Yes, I was.'

'Well, it would be a natural sequence of thought at the end of the day which marks the end of an old life and the beginning of a new one. Do you want to talk about it?'

'Our new life? It will be strange—for me, at least. I shall have to learn Dutch, won't I? Is your home here anything like the house you've bought in London?'

'Er—no. For one thing it is in the country, on the edge of a small village near a lake. It is very convenient for me. I go to Utrecht as well as Leiden, and from time to time Amsterdam.'

'Will we be coming back to Holland in a little while?'

'Yes. I'll be in London and travelling around the

country for several weeks, and then we'll be back here for several months—although I quite often go over to England for a few days if something turns up where I'm needed.'

'Do you go to other countries?'

'From time to time. The States and the Middle East—usually to see private patients—and occasionally to Germany and Italy.'

He glanced at her quiet profile. 'It will be nice to have someone to come home to in future,' he told her.

That warmed her heart.

Once they had crossed into Holland, Gijs picked up the carphone. 'I'll let them know we're expecting supper when we arrive home,' he told her. She wondered who 'they' were.

The motorways were good and there were no hills and almost no corners; there was nothing to hinder the car's speed. They skirted Rotterdam and sped on to Utrecht to turn away from that city and go north towards Soest. There was a fitful moon, peering from time to time from billowing clouds, and Margo could see that they had left the flat grassland behind and that the country upon either side of the road was thick with trees and bushes.

'Is this a forest?'

'Not exactly—woods and undergrowth and heath. Hilversum is to the north and Amersfoot to the east— both quite large towns. We turn off here.'

He drove along a narrow country road, the woods on either side broken from time to time by great gateways, and presently slowed to enter a small village, its houses ringed around a church. 'Arntzstein,' said the professor quietly. 'Our home is here.'

He swept through the village, past some elegant houses with lights streaming from their uncurtained windows, and into a narrow lane which ended in an open gateway flanked by stone pillars. The drive was short, curving in a semicircle to the wide sweep before the house at its end.

Margo, blinking at the lighted windows, began to count them and gave up.

'You don't live here?' she asked in a worried voice.

'*We* live here,' he corrected her quietly. 'Yes, this is our home, Margo.'

He got out and opened her door and she stood on the wide sweep, looking at the house.

It was four storeys high, with a gabled roof and a small round tower at each end. Its windows, tall and narrow on the ground floor, decreased in size at each level, the topmost of them being dormer windows set in the gable...

Margo took a deep breath. 'Well—you might have told me, Gijs.'

He took her arm. 'No. No—you would have rejected me instantly as being highly unsuitable. Come and have your supper. You must be tired—it's been a long day.'

Not just a long day, she thought, climbing the double stone stairs to the massive front door, our wedding day.

It was opened as they reached it by a stout elderly man with a jolly face.

'Wim.' The professor spoke to the man in his own language, shaking his hand, and then said in English, 'Margo, this is Wim, who runs this place. His wife is housekeeper; you will meet her presently. Wim speaks English.'

Margo shook hands and smiled at the beaming face.

'Welcome, *mevrouw*. It is with pleasure that we see you.' He stood aside and waved an arm towards the entrance hall, where there were several people standing. 'If it is permitted...'

The professor took her arm and they crossed the black and white tiled floor. Margo was led from one person to the next: Wim's wife, Kieke, Jet, the housemaid, Diny and Mien, the cooks. There was also an elderly man, wizened and wrinkled with the weather, and the professor clapped him on the shoulder and wrung his hand. 'Willem, who has looked after the gardens ever since I can remember.'

She shook each one by the hand and murmured greetings, glad of their friendly faces, and presently she was led away up a carved oak staircase to her room.

'Don't do more than take off your hat and coat,' the professor called after her. 'Supper's waiting.'

She had no time to do more than glance at the room Kieke ushered her into. It was a lovely room, its tall windows draped in old rose brocade, with the same brocade covering the vast bed with its satinwood headboard. The dressing table was satinwood too, with a triple mirror on it and a padded stool, covered in tapestry, before it. There were two small easy chairs covered in a darker pink, and a chaise longue at the foot of the bed upholstered in ivory velvet.

Margo heaved a sigh of pure pleasure and at the same time thought how impractical the furnishings were; she would be afraid to sit on anything for fear of spoiling it. She poked at her hair, powdered her nose and went downstairs to find Gijs waiting for her in the hall.

'Your room is all right?' he wanted to know. 'Do tell Wim if there is anything you want.' He led the way across the hall into a panelled room hung with portraits. There was an oval table at its centre, ringed by mahogany chairs of the Chippendale period, and against a wall a sideboard of the same period. There was a corner cupboard, its door of marquetry, and a splendid fireplace with a marble surround in which a bright fire burned. Crimson velvet curtains were drawn across the windows and there were fine rugs on the polished wood floor.

Supper was hardly the meal she had expected. One end of the table had been set with lace mats, silver and crystal, gleaming under the light from a chiselled bronze chandelier. She sat down opposite Gijs.

'You have a beautiful home,' she observed. 'I had no idea…it's like being married to a millionaire…' She smiled at him, and then took a quick breath at the look on his face. 'Oh, you're not, are you?'

'Well, yes, I am. But don't let it worry you, Margo. I have never allowed it to worry me. Perhaps I should have told you…'

'If you had, I don't think I would have married you.'

'In that case I'm glad I kept silent.' He smiled suddenly. 'Am I forgiven?'

'Well, of course—and I dare say I'll get used to it in time.' She spooned her soup. 'I can hear a dog barking…'

'Punch. He was out when we arrived. He knows we are here.'

'Is he allowed in here? What breed is he?'

'He goes all over the house. He's a bloodhound.'

The professor said something to Wim, who went away and presently returned with Punch, who lolloped across the room to greet his master and, when bidden to do so, offered his noble head to be scratched by Margo.

'He's lovely—how you must miss him.'

'Indeed I do.' The professor began to talk about his dog, also mentioning that Kieke had two cats. 'And there are rabbits here, of course, and hares and squirrels…' He talked easily as they ate turbot and winter salad and a Dutch apple tart and cream. 'And since it is an occasion,' said Gijs smoothly, 'we will drink champagne...'

It was late by the time they rose from the table and crossed the hall again to enter the drawing room. This was a splendid apartment, with a massive fireplace in front of which Punch instantly settled himself. There were two chandeliers here, one at each end of the room, but the only lighting came from wall-lights and table-lamps so that the room was dimly lit.

Margo, by now too sleepy to examine her surroundings, drank her coffee and looked across at Gijs with owl-like eyes.

'You're tired,' he said, and got to his feet. 'Stay in bed tomorrow morning if you would like that—Diny will bring your breakfast.'

'I'd rather come down, if you don't mind. It's just that it has been a busy sort of day.'

She waited for him to say something—something about being married and liking it, or what a pleasant wedding it had been. He didn't—only wished her good-night with the hope that she would sleep well.

At the door, which he opened for her, he bent and kissed her cheek. A brotherly peck, reflected Margo peevishly, and was instantly sorry for the thought. What else had she expected?

In her room she prowled around, looking at everything—someone had unpacked and hung her few clothes in the big mirror-lined closet, the bed had been turned down and there was a light on in the bathroom. There was everything here that a girl could wish for: fluffy towels, creams and lotions and bath salts. She opened the door in the far wall and poked a cautious head round. This was Gijs's room, she supposed. Quite small and comfortably furnished. She closed the door

again and went to take another look at her own room.
There were books by the bed and a tin of biscuits, as
well as a handsome carafe of water. Tomorrow, she
decided, she would write Aunt Flo a long letter and tell
her all about it.

Presently she undressed, had a bath and got into bed,
and, despite the thoughts tumbling around in her tired
head, slept at once.

As she went down the staircase the following morning
she was delighted to see a Christmas tree in one corner
of the hall, and as she reached the last stair Gijs and
Punch came in through the front door, bringing a breath
of icy air with them.

His good morning was cheerful. 'You slept well?
Good. Come and have breakfast. It's cold but fine outside.'

'The tree...' said Margo.

'We will decorate it when we get back this afternoon.
The children expect it, you know.'

'Children?'

'My sisters will be coming tomorrow, with their husbands and children. The family always hold Christmas
here.'

He had her arm and was urging her into a small room
at the back of the hall. A small table was laid there and
the fire burned cheerfully. He pulled out a chair for her
and Wim came in with the coffee-pot.

'I thought we might go into Utrecht this morning,'
said the professor placidly. 'Christmas presents—we've
left it a bit late, but you will know what to buy.'

Margo was still finding her tongue. She said now,
rather coldly, 'I haven't the faintest idea what I am to
buy. I—I didn't expect all this...' she waved a hand

around the room '…this magnificence. I thought you were just a surgeon.'

'I am just a surgeon. If you can't bear to live here we'll close the place up and go and live in a very small cottage.'

'Don't be absurd,' said Margo, and felt laughter bubbling up inside her. 'How long have you lived here?'

'Just over two hundred years.'

'Well…' She did laugh then. 'I feel as though I've walked into a fairy tale.' She added, serious now, 'But I don't know anything about the presents you want me to buy.'

He said soothingly, 'No, no, of course you don't. But if I tell you for whom each one is you might choose them. I never know what to buy for my sisters.'

'Oh, well, is Utrecht far? Perhaps I *could* help.'

'Five or six miles away. There is a large shopping centre there. We can have lunch out and be back here in the afternoon in time to decorate the tree.' He passed his cup for more coffee. 'Have you phoned Aunt Florence?'

'I got up and dressed and came downstairs and now I'm eating my breakfast. I've not been given the chance to do anything else.'

'Am I rushing you? I don't mean to, but to tell the truth you have accepted everything in such a matter-of-fact manner that I forget that it is all strange to you.' He smiled at her across the table. 'This evening after dinner we will sit quietly together and I will answer all your questions and explain anything you want me to.'

'Yes, I'd like that. Have I time to ring Aunt Flo before we go to Utrecht?'

'Of course.' He glanced at the long-case clock against the wall. 'Twenty minutes.' He got up with her.

'There's a phone in the library; no one will disturb you there.'

He led the way through the hall and opened a door. It was a beautiful room, with a plastered ceiling, shelves of books on its walls and several small tables with comfortable chairs beside them, and at one end of the room was a vast desk. He picked up the phone on it and dialled Aunt Florence's number, handed it to her and went away, leaving her to give her aunt a garbled version of their journey and the house.

'I can't stop to tell you everything,' said Margo. 'We're just off to Utrecht to buy presents. But, Aunt Flo, it's all so magnificent. I'll phone you this evening and tell you all about it.'

'You're happy, Margo?'

'Yes, Aunt Flo...'

'Run along, then, and tell me the rest this evening.'

Margo got into her winter coat, feeling doubtful about wearing it. Her wedding outfit would be too thin, though, and besides, she hadn't time to change from her skirt and sweater and she had no hat. She went downstairs, very conscious that her clothes were not at all right for the wife of a well-known surgeon.

The professor thought the same thing, but nothing of the thought showed on his face. In any case, it was something which could be put right quite easily. They went out to the car with Punch and drove away, with Wim watching them benignly from the porch.

Utrecht looked magnificent, decided Margo presently, staring out of the car window as Gijs drove through a bewildering succession of streets to park. Then, accompanied by Punch on his lead, he led her down a narrow alley and into an enormous shopping precinct.

'Have you brought a list with you?' asked Margo,

pausing to look in the window of an elegant jeweller. 'What heavenly shops…'

'Presently.' He took her arm and ushered her into the kind of boutique she had so often looked into and never dared to enter.

'Why—?' began Margo. Surely she wasn't supposed to choose clothes for his sisters?

It seemed that she was to choose clothes for herself. She listened, speechless, while he spoke to the haughty-looking woman who came to meet them. The haughtiness vanished when she saw him. They shook hands, then she patted Punch's noble head and said in excellent English, 'It will be a pleasure to dress you, Mevrouw van Kessel. What did you have in mind?'

Her sharp eyes had taken in the elderly coat and the sensible shoes—fit, in her opinion, for the dustbin.

Margo gave the professor a thoughtful look and he said placidly, 'My Christmas present to you, my dear. Shall we start with something warm—a dress, perhaps?'

It was no sooner said than done. Dresses were produced—fine wool, jersey, cashmere… Margo, still speechless, tried them on and couldn't decide which one she liked best. She showed herself to Gijs in each of them, and when she asked which he preferred he said carelessly, 'The brown jersey and the blue cashmere; have them both.'

'Thank you, Gijs…'

Before she could say more he went on, 'A winter coat and a tweed suit?'

He lifted an eyebrow at the saleslady, who said, 'I have just the thing. Brown cashmere—so warm and light—and there is a suit in greens and blues which will become her very well.'

She disappeared into an enormous closet at the back

of the shop and Margo hissed, 'Gijs, you can't—everything's frightfully expensive; you have no idea.'

'Ah, but it is Christmas, Margo. Try them on to please me.'

The coat fitted and so did the suit. '*Mevrouw* has an exact size ten and a charming figure. If I might suggest a hat…'

The professor nodded. 'Very nice. I'm going to take Punch for a quick walk, and while I am gone you are to choose dresses for the evening. We are very festive at Christmas, so something pretty for the afternoon and a couple of dresses for the evening—we have friends in and I intend you to be the belle of the ball.'

Margo found her tongue. 'I can't think what to say…'

'Then don't.' He smiled at her. 'And don't dare ask the price. Remember this is my Christmas present to you.'

He went away then, and she was led away to the cubicle once again. And, since Gijs wished her to look as elegant as possible, she spent a long time choosing between a dark green velvet dress with a wide sweeping skirt and what she considered to be a very immodest neckline and a wine-red taffeta dress with a tucked bodice and long, tight sleeves.

'I think Professor van Kessel intended you to have two dresses, *mevrouw*,' suggested the saleslady.

Margo remembered that he *had* said 'a couple'. She nodded cheerful agreement and turned her attention to something pretty for the afternoon. Turning this way and that, to examine the excellent fit of a Paisley-patterned silk dress, she observed that she already had the other dresses. Surely they would do?

The saleslady shook her head. 'I have the pleasure of dressing the professor's sisters from time to time—

you will wish to look as elegantly dressed as they will be, *mevrouw*. Also, he wished it.'

An irrefutable argument. Margo handed the dress over to be wrapped up and got back into her skirt and woolly.

'Perhaps *mevrouw* would like to wear the coat?' suggested the saleslady. 'So much easier than packing it—and of course the hat.'

Studying her reflection in the cubicle's enormous mirror, Margo had to admit that clothes did make a difference. She adjusted the hat just so and went back into the shop.

Gijs was there, sitting with Punch like a statue beside him. He got up as she crossed the thick carpet. 'You found what you liked, I hope? Good. We'll have coffee, and when we've done our shopping we'll collect the parcels from here.'

He turned to speak to the saleslady, who smiled and nodded and shook hands again. 'I hope that I shall see you again, *mevrouw*.'

Margo beamed at her. 'I'm most grateful for your help and advice. I like everything, and I know I shall enjoy wearing the dresses.'

They had coffee then, in a bustling café with a giant Christmas tree. It was crowded with customers, several of whom came over to their table to greet the professor—large, self-assured men with their wives and sometimes children whom he introduced to her, uttering names she instantly forgot. They all spoke English and her shyness melted before their kind smiles.

They would meet again, they all assured her, when next Gijs came to Holland. She felt a glow of pleasure at the thought.

They bought the presents next, from a long list. No one was forgotten: Willem had a box of cigars and a corduroy waistcoat; Diny had a vividly patterned sweater. And when Margo asked doubtfully if she would like it Gijs told her that Kieke had been shopping with Diny and she had admired it. His sisters, he mentioned, wore earrings, so they spent time in the jeweller's spending what Margo secretly feared was a small fortune.

When they finally got to the end of the list, he took her to the Café de Paris where they had roast pheasant and an almond tart with lashings of cream while Punch sat silent beside his master, accepting the odd morsel with quiet dignity.

Somehow, and Margo wasn't sure how it happened, she then found herself in a luxurious shoe shop, trying on soft leather boots, shoes so soft and supple that she hardly knew she had them on her feet and evening shoes, high-heeled and strappy.

She emerged rather pink in the face, and, on the way to the car stopped suddenly to say, 'Thank you very much Gijs. You have bought me so many lovely things. I have enough clothes for several years.'

He stood looking down at her, smiling a little. 'I had no idea that dressing my wife would be such fun; you must allow me the pleasure of doing it as often as I like. I can hardly wait to get to Harrods when we get back to London.'

The pink deepened, and it struck him that she wasn't a plain girl at all.

'Well,' said Margo, rather at a loss for words, 'I must say it's lovely to have so many clothes all at once.' She put a hand on his arm. 'Gijs, will you change some money for me? I mean, I've got some English pounds with me but I want some *gulden*.'

'Of course. How much would you like?' His matter-of-fact manner made it easy for her.

'About twenty-five pounds.'

He took some notes out of his wallet. 'You can give me twenty-five pounds when we get home. That's the equivalent in *gulden*.'

'Thank you—would you mind waiting here? They'll understand English?'

'Oh, yes. We'll be here.'

She hurried across the complex to a small shop they had stopped to look at. Gijs had admired a folding leather photo frame, remarking how useful it would be for anyone who travelled a good deal. It was a paltry gift compared with those which he had lavished upon her, but at least it was something he might use. She entered the shop, bought it and rejoined him, flushed with success.

The parcels and packages collected and stowed in the boot, they drove back to Arntzstein to tea round the fire and then the pleasurable task of decorating the tree.

Because she felt happy and the house was so beautiful, Margo changed into the velvet skirt and blouse and trod downstairs in Aunt Flo's slippers.

Gijs had changed too, into one of his sober dark grey suits. He was waiting for her in the drawing room with Punch beside him.

Margo said awkwardly, 'I'm saving my new dresses for tomorrow and Christmas Day. Will your sisters be here early tomorrow?'

'Teatime—there will be friends coming in for drinks and we shall dine late, I expect.' He crossed the room and took her hand. 'You are the mistress of our home now, Margo, but it hardly seems fair to expect you to organise everything. Wim and Kieke have been here for years and know the whole set-up. I think that she would be flattered if you went to the kitchen tomorrow morning and have a talk—she will expect you to take over when you're ready. Wim will be there to translate.'

She said gravely, 'Yes, of course. I'd like to get to know her and find out how the house is run. I hope I won't be a disappointment to you, Gijs.'

'I am quite certain that you will never be that, my dear. Now come and have a drink, and after dinner we'll go round the house together.' He bent and kissed her cheek. 'I have thrown you in at the deep end, haven't I?' He laughed a little. 'I know you will cope admirably, though.'

'Because I am the vicar's daughter...?'

'Why, yes.'

If that's a compliment, reflected Margo, I must be thankful for it.

CHAPTER SEVEN

FEELING self-conscious, Margo went down to breakfast in the new tweed suit, and was instantly reassured by Gijs's look of approval. They breakfasted then, talking about the preparations for the following day.

'I must go down to the village this morning,' he told her, 'but you will be discussing things with Kieke, no doubt, and I'll be back in time for us to take Punch for a walk before lunch.'

She agreed happily. He had told her a great deal about his family on the previous evening, and taken her on a tour of the house, lingering in each room so that she could examine it to her heart's content. She had loved every moment—going through the beautiful old house, looking at the furniture with which Gijs had grown up, examining photos of his parents and family, listening to the snippets of information he'd told her. She had the feeling now, facing him over the breakfast table, that they had become a little closer to each other. Even the house didn't seem strange—it was as though it had accepted her as its new mistress...!

So, apparently, had Kieke and Wim. In the vast kitchen she was seated at the scrubbed tale and the household books were laid before her. It had been the custom, said Wim, for him to make up the household accounts and present them to his master when he returned home, but now, of course, *mevrouw* would attend to the matter and Kieke would be happy to discuss menus and the buying of provisions if *mevrouw* would come each morning to the kitchen.

'Yes, of course I will—if that is what Mevrouw van Kessel always did. But I know nothing about the running of a large house and I hope that you and Kieke will help me. I'll learn to speak Dutch as soon as possible. We shall be back in a month or so.' She smiled at his good-natured face. 'You and Kieke will forgive me if I get things wrong?'

A remark which earned their entire approval. Here was a young lady who would, under their guidance, become a worthy mistress of the ancestral home.

As teatime approached Margo because increasingly nervous. She had got into the cashmere dress and a pair of the new shoes, done her face and hair with the kind of close attention she rarely bestowed upon them, and now she was in the drawing room, sitting uneasily opposite Gijs. She found it annoying that he could sit there, completely at his ease, with Punch lying across his feet, reading *de Haagse Dagblad*, for all the world as though it weren't Christmas Eve with guests arriving at any minute.

'You don't need to be nervous,' he said, without looking up from his reading. 'You must have faced many a Mothers' Union meeting and attended untold village gatherings.' He glanced at her then. 'You look very nice.'

A crumb of comfort, she supposed. If he had been in love with her, she reflected, he would have said that she was lovely or beautiful, because love was blind, wasn't it? Looking nice was better than looking dowdy, however, she comforted herself, and sat up very straight at the sound of cars approaching and then a medley of voices.

The professor put down his newspaper, removed his feet from under Punch and stood up. He plucked Margo gently from her chair, put an arm through hers and walked her into the hall.

It was full of people, all talking at once, with children darting here and there and Wim and Diny taking coats and scarves. There was a rush towards them as they came out of the drawing room and Margo found herself embraced in turn by three young women and then three husbands, and last of all by Gijs's brother, a younger version of him, with his features and blue eyes but not his great height. Margo, with a string of names nicely muddled in her head, bent to greet the children. There were eight of them—four girls and four boys—the youngest a toddler, the eldest rising twelve.

'You poor dear!' exclaimed one of the sisters. 'We are swamping you—it is not good that we should come and stay when you are just married. However, Gijs will not alter the family custom. You do not mind?' She smiled at Margo. 'I'm Lise, the eldest. Franz is my husband, and Marcus and Jan and Minna are our children. Did Gijs not tell you our names?'

'Well, there hasn't been much time, but it's lovely meeting you all like this, and I'm so relieved that you all speak English. Even the children...'

'We have a Scottish nanny—all the children have a small knowledge. You are exactly as Gijs described you. We will be friends—and my sisters also.'

'I shall like that. Would you like to go to your rooms first or come into the drawing room for tea?'

'You do not mind if the children are with us?'

'Of course not. Christmas isn't Christmas without children, is it?'

'And you will perhaps have added to them by next Christmas,' Franz said as he joined them.

Margo went pink and Lise said comfortably, 'Take

no notice of him, Margo; he is a great tease. I think we will go to our rooms, if we may, and then tea.'

Margo led the way upstairs, ushering everyone into their rooms, sorting out the children, making sure that Nanny had all she wanted. Nanny was a quiet little woman who could have been any age between forty and fifty.

'You'll come down for tea,' said Margo. 'I expect you know the house better than I do, so please do exactly as you've always done.'

'Aye, *mevrouw*, I've been with the family since Minna was born—she's the eldest of the children.' She smiled suddenly. 'I'll wish you happy, you and the professor; it's time he was wed.'

Margo went back downstairs and found the men settled by the fire. They all got up as she went in.

'Oh, please don't get up. I'll see about tea.'

She whispered herself out of the room. Gijs had been right; she was on familiar ground. It wasn't the Mothers' Union, but she had had years of meeting people and making them feel at home, listening while they talked, seeing that they had food and drink.

Much later, getting ready for bed, she decided that so far everything had gone well. The house had absorbed their guests into its numerous rooms and she thought the children had behaved beautifully, gathering round the lighted tree before going up to what had once been the nursery to have their supper and go to bed.

There had been a great deal of to-ing and fro-ing, but eventually everyone had gathered in the drawing room for drinks—the men in black tie and the women in long dresses. Margo, in the green velvet and still not sure about the low-cut neck, had nevertheless lost her shyness and apprehension and been the perfect hostess.

Dinner had been leisurely, and it had been late when they'd gone back to the drawing room for coffee.

'There are a few friends coming in later for a drink,' Gijs had said. 'I suggest we put the presents round the tree before they get here.'

There had been a good deal of bustle then, with stealthy creeping upstairs to fetch gaily wrapped gifts and a lot of laughing. She had laid her present for Gijs with the others round the tree and then slipped away to make sure that everyone in the kitchen had had their supper.

Kieke had beamed at her praise for dinner and Wim had assured her that he would be bringing in drinks and canapés in preparation for the visitors who would be calling in presently.

'A very happy Christmas, *mevrouw*,' he had chuckled. 'Everyone is happy.'

The guests had arrived soon after, and she had been so pleased to see Beatrice and her husband. There hadn't been time to talk much but they had arranged to try and meet in Utrecht before Margo went back to England. She had enjoyed herself then, going from one to the other with Gijs, shaking hands, being kissed and congratulated.

A dream, she told herself now, curling up in bed—a dream from which she would have to wake up once Christmas was over and Gijs was back in London, wrapped up in his work. She would make a home for him, she promised herself, and be there when he wanted her and make no fuss when he had to go away...

She slept, for it was one o'clock in the morning and tomorrow was Christmas Day and she wanted to be up early.

It was a day to remember for the rest of her life! The noisy, cheerful breakfast, then church, where she was confident that she looked her best in her new coat and hat and even the carols were sung to familiar tunes, then back to the house for turkey and Christmas pudding.

Just as though we're in England, she reflected, pulling crackers with the children, unaware that Gijs had gone to a good deal of trouble to see that it was. Presently they gathered round the tree and the presents were handed out by Gijs, starting with the smallest child.

There were parcels for her too—not just one or two but a pile of gaily coloured gifts: a silk scarf from a famous fashion house, an evening bag, gloves, a wide leather belt, chocolates, a leather travelling clock. She went round thanking everyone, and when she got to Gijs he put a long jewellers' case into her hand. 'To mark our first Christmas together,' he told her, and bent to kiss her.

There were pearls inside—a very beautiful necklace with a sapphire and diamond clasp. He fastened them round her neck and she leaned up to kiss him. 'But I've had my presents,' she reminded him. 'They are lovely...'

He flung an arm round her shoulder. 'Now you're here, I'll open your present,' he announced. 'Just what I wanted,' he told her moments later. 'We must have your photo taken...'

He kissed her again, the light, cool kiss she had come to expect from him and must learn to accept. For the time being, she reminded herself. She loved him and surely in time he would learn to love her.

Everyone gathered in the drawing room for tea, and when it had been cleared away the furniture was moved to leave a great space in the centre of the room and they played games with the children—Musical Chairs, Grandmother's Footsteps, Blind Man's Bluff. And Margo, caught in Gijs's great arms with everyone shouting at him to guess who it was, forgot herself so far as to murmur, 'Oh, Gijs,' against his vast chest. Heaven knew what she might have added, but, of course, he guessed and released her...

The children, calmed with supper, were put to bed, and everyone else went away to change for the evening. Margo, lying in the bath, decided to wear the taffeta. The pearls would look lovely with it, and it was delightful to dress up...

There was no one else in the drawing room but Gijs when she went down. He was standing in front of the fire, Punch beside him, immaculate in black tie. He and his house suited each other, thought Margo. She said out loud, 'How can you bear to be away from this house, Gijs?'

He smiled. 'Come and sit down. How very nice you look. As for going away, I go because my work is important to me—part of my life, something I must do. Now that I'm married I shall return home each time with even greater pleasure.'

'You like living in England?'

'Certainly I do. When we go back to London we must set about getting the house furnished as quickly as possible. I dare say you already have some ideas?'

'Well, no. There have been so many other things to think about. But I will—can't we do it together?'

She saw the look of faint impatience on his face.

'Whenever I am free, by all means. There are some rather nice pieces in the attic here. We will have a look at them before we return and I'll have whatever we think will fit in sent over.'

The first of their guests joined them then, and there

was no more chance to talk together that evening. Nor would there be tomorrow, she remembered: Boxing Day—only they called it the Second Christmas Day in Holland—and they were all going to the village to a party for the children there. Another tradition, she supposed, and a nice one.

The party was fun, with everyone taking part in the games. There was a table laden with soft drinks, cakes and biscuits, oranges and nuts, and in one corner of the village hall a stall serving *potat frits,* hot and crisp with a dollop of pickles in paper pokes. There was a Christmas tree, of course, and every child there had a present from it.

Margo, helping Gijs hand them out, felt quite at home; she had done the same thing for years at Thinbottom. That evening there were more callers, staying for drinks, so that they dined late.

'You do have a great many friends,' said Margo when she had a moment alone with Gijs.

'They came to see the bride.'

'Well, I dare say they were surprised that you'd got married. I expect I was a bit of a surprise.'

He agreed blandly and she suspected that he was amused, although she wasn't sure why. Probably they had expected an elegant beauty; despite the pretty dresses and the careful hairdo she would never be other than herself. Ordinary.

Everyone went away after breakfast the next morning, and the house seemed very quiet and empty. Margo had a painstaking session in the kitchen with Kieke then went in search of Gijs. A walk would be nice; it was cold and frosty but now and again there was a glimmer of sunshine. They could talk—get to know each other better...

He was in his study when she poked her head round the door, his handsome nose buried in a pile of papers. He looked up as she went in, but she said, 'Don't get up—I can see you're busy.'

'A chance to get some work done without the phone ringing every few minutes. I dare say you can amuse yourself until lunchtime?'

She swallowed disappointment and the beginnings of temper. Surely on holiday he could spare time to be with her? She said, a shade too heartily, 'Oh, yes. Would you like Wim to bring your coffee in here?'

She waited to see if he would suggest that they have it together. His vague, 'Yes, yes, that would be splendid. Off you go and enjoy yourself,' made it obvious that he had no such idea.

She went away quietly, conscious that he was hardly aware of her going.

She went to her room, got into the cashmere coat, tied a scarf over her head, found shoes and gloves, and went downstairs to find Wim.

'I'm going for a walk, Wim. I haven't seen the gardens properly. Don't tell the professor—he's working and mustn't be disturbed. If you'd take his coffee in presently...?'

'And you, *mevrouw*? Your coffee?'

'I'll have it when I get back. It's such a lovely day and I have so much to see.'

She gave his anxious face a reassuring smile and went through the door he held open for her and down the steps.

She explored the garden, which was much larger than she had thought, and then, still feeling put out, went down the drive and out of the gate. She didn't go to the village—she knew where that was and had had a glimpse of it yesterday—but instead took the other direction along the narrow lane bordered by the high walls of Gijs's garden and then by straggling bushes which in turn became open fields.

It was cold. She hadn't realised how cold until she'd started walking in the open country. There were no hills, but flat, orderly meadows bisected by canals, already iced over. There was no one and nothing in sight either, though presently she saw a church steeple and a cluster of cottages. Another village—and she was sure she could see a glimpse of water. Gijs had told her that there were lakes nearby.

She walked on, wishing that she had had coffee before she'd left the house. But away from the house she could think... It was early days, she told herself; she would need a great deal of patience. Gijs was used to being a bachelor. When they got back to London she would set about making a home for them both and at the same time learn to make the best of herself.

A good hairdresser? A visit to a beauty parlour, perhaps? More clothes? And she must find something to keep her occupied so that he need never feel guilty about leaving her alone. A baby crêche, perhaps, or helping at a playschool. At the same time she would learn to be a good hostess and housewife.

Uplifted by these ambitious thoughts, she walked on, and presently, seeing a side-lane and a glint of water beyond, turned down it. There were a few bushes and small trees near the water. There was a small jetty too, and a couple of small boats hauled up on the bank. The water looked cold and grey, and a nasty mean wind was ruffling it.

Margo shivered, and looked around her, suddenly aware that the sky had become dark. She had walked further than she had intended; she glanced at her watch and was surprised to see that in half an hour it would be lunchtime. She started back along the lane as the first soft flakes of snow began to fall. By the time she reached the other lane, it was falling in a thick curtain, turning the surrounding countryside into a formless white blanket.

'A good thing that it's a straight road,' said Margo, her voice sounding loud in the silence. She walked on, her head bent against the blinding snow, unaware that she had gone off the road and that ahead of her were a series of narrow canals, already concealed under the snow...

It was Wim who began to worry as the snow started. He took a large umbrella and went round the gardens calling her, looking in the various out-houses where she might be sheltering. There was no sign of her, and he went back to the kitchen.

'There is no sign of *mevrouw*,' he told Kieke. 'Perhaps she came in without saying anything and is in her room...'

It was Diny who spoke. '*Mevrouw*? I saw her go out of the gate with my own eyes not an hour ago.'

Gijs didn't lift his head from his work as Wim knocked and went in.

'*Mevrouw* has gone out, *mijnheer*, and it is snowing hard.'

The professor was on his feet in an instant. 'Did she say where she was going?' He went to look out of the window then strode into the hall, followed by Punch. 'I'll go after her—she must have gone to the village. Phone the shop there and ask if anyone has seen her, will you, Wim?'

He was getting into his Barbour jacket and taking off

his shoes as he spoke. Kieke, who had come into the hall, went without a word and fetched his rubber boots, then thrust a woollen scarf at him. 'Put that in your pocket, *mijnheer. Mevrouw* will be cold.'

Wim reported that no one had seen her in the village although she might be there, visiting, perhaps. It didn't seem likely. It was a small place where everyone knew everyone else's business; if she had been there someone would have known about it.

'If she returns before I'm back,' said the professor, 'get her into a warm bath and bed, Kieke.' He whistled to Punch, nodded to Wim and left his house.

There was only one other way to go, he reasoned, if Margo hadn't gone to the village, and that was along the lane leading to the next village and the lakes.

Once he had passed his own walls and then the few trees he paused to shout before going on again. He had walked for ten minutes or more, pausing to bellow her name, when there was a lull in the storm and the snow thinned, giving him a chance to look around him. He saw her at once, going slowly across the fields. She had stopped to look around her and he began to run, and when he saw her starting to walk again he shouted, 'Stand still, Margo. Don't move.'

She was so surprised, she almost fell over, but she obeyed him and he fetched up beside her, breathing hard, and not altogether because he had been running. All the same his voice was quiet. 'Just in time,' he told her placidly. 'You were rather near a canal.'

He took the scarf off her head and tied the woolly one on instead. She gave a sniff. 'I got a bit lost,' she said in a voice she strove to keep matter-of-fact. 'I didn't expect it to snow quite so hard.'

He took her arm. 'We'll get home before it starts

again.' He saw her mouth shaking. 'Punch is so pleased to have found you; he's your slave already.'

He was walking her back to the road, and as they reached it the snow started to fall again. He put an arm around her shoulders and held her close. 'We might get lost again,' said Margo in a small voice.

'Not with Punch leading the way.' She felt his arm tighten. 'This is my fault, Margo. I should never have left you alone. I'm sorry. I have become selfish living on my own—I—'

She interrupted him. 'Of course you're not selfish— what a silly notion. And it wasn't your fault. You weren't to know that I was going out or that it was going to snow. Silly of me not to have told Wim...'

Punch gave a cheerful bark as they turned in at the gate, and ran ahead of them and through the door Wim already had open, to shake himself all over the hall floor then lope into the drawing room to flop before the fire. No one reprimanded him; they were too busy getting out of encrusted coats, and kicking off wet shoes and boots while the professor gave quiet and unhurried instructions.

Margo, escorted upstairs by Kieke, had a hot bath prescribed for her, and then, once more warm and dry in a sweater and skirt, went back downstairs.

There was no one in the drawing room, and although the table was laid for lunch in the dining room there was no one there either. She was standing in the hall, wondering if she should go to Gijs's study, when he opened the door of the small sitting room at the back of the hall.

'There you are. Come in and have a drink; it's cosy here. You're none the worse for your adventure?'

He pulled a small easy chair forward and gave her a glass of sherry.

'I have to go to Utrecht in the morning—would you like to come with me? There are some splendid shops and you know your way around there now. I'll meet you for lunch.'

'I'd like that. Perhaps I could find something to take back to Aunt Flo.'

They lunched together, and then went up to the attic where she poked around, delighted at the chairs and tables, sofas and tallboys stored there.

'You could furnish a whole house...'

'You like the idea? Good. Pick out what you want—there must be enough here to furnish several rooms.'

She wanted almost everything. 'This—and this. Oh, and this...'

She stopped to look at an old-fashioned cradle on rockers. On her knees, she examined it carefully. 'It's very old, isn't it? Hasn't it been used for a long time?'

'Good lord, yes. All the van Kessels spend the first month or so in it. 'It's very comfortable, I've been told.' He smiled down at her, amused at her eagerness. 'I can't remember if that is so.'

She stood up and went to look at a little table inlaid with mother-of-pearl, conscious that her face was red and desperately unhappy because it hadn't meant anything to him. Didn't he want children? He had said that he wanted a wife and perhaps that was all he did want—someone to run his house, be a hostess to his friends, be there when he came home...

They went to Utrecht soon after breakfast the next day, with Punch sitting, as usual, on the back seat.

'I'll put you down at the shopping precinct,' Gijs told her. 'You remember the small enclosure in the centre, with the seats round it? I'll meet you there at half past twelve.' He glanced at his watch. 'I'm sorry I haven't time to have coffee with you, but I'm already late.'

'I'll be there,' she told him, and wondered where he was going.

She had coffee and then began her search for a present for Aunt Flo. She had money now; Gijs had put some notes into her purse with the remark that she might see something she wanted to buy and she counted them now. There was enough money to buy the kitchen stove if she'd wanted to.

She strolled round, looking in the shop windows, which were still for the most part filled with Christmas merchandise. She found a silk scarf in misty greys and blues that would be the very thing for Aunt Flo, and then, since she had so much money, bought a gold scarf pin to go with it. Her aunt loved chocolates, she remembered, and so bought a splendid box tied with ribbons and filled with mouthwatering confections, loaded with calories.

Her purchases in an elegant carrier bag, she had another cup of coffee, made sure that her hair and face were as near to perfection as possible, and wandered back to the shops once more. Almost at once her eye was caught by a small, silver-plated calendar—just the thing for Gijs's desk. He had given her so much, and the leather photo frame had been paltry compared with all the magnificent presents she had received. She bought it and had it wrapped in pretty paper then put it with her other purchases. By then it was almost half past twelve.

It was quite warm with the lighted shops all around her and people hurrying to and fro, and she hardly noticed the time passing. Finally, a clock somewhere striking the hour disturbed her thoughts. Gijs was late.

Perhaps she had misunderstood him? But there was only one enclosure...

By half past one she was not only worried, she was cross too. Here I am, she fumed silently, in a foreign country; I don't even know the phone number at Arntzstein or how to get there. I don't know where he is. I might still be here when the shops close. He's forgotten me. He's forgotten that he's married! Probably drinking with his pals.

She knew that the last assumption was nonsense, but she felt better for thinking it. Just let him come now, and she would tell him how tiresome he was.

'I'm sorry I kept you waiting,' said Gijs from behind her.

She spun round. 'An hour—more than an hour—I've been sitting here. If I'd known where to go I'd have gone.' She took a heaving breath. 'It's not even England...'

His mouth twitched but he answered her gravely. 'I know. Tear me apart if you want to. I hadn't forgotten you, though.'

'Then why didn't you come when you said you would?'

She uttered the words which came so readily to wives the world over. 'Where have you been?'

He came and sat down beside her then. 'I had no idea I would be so long. I went to the hospital to see who they had put on my waiting list and a child was admitted while I was there. She needed surgery—my kind of surgery...'

Her peevishness evaporated. 'Gijs, I'm sorry I was cross. What a mess I'm making of being your wife. Of course doctors' wives expect to get left, don't they? And they don't grumble. I won't do it again, I promise.'

'I must remember to tell you if I'm going to be late

home too.' He spoke lightly. 'Although I don't always know.'

'Friends?' asked Margo, holding out a hand.

He shook it. 'Friends for life,' he assured her.

They had their lunch then in perfect harmony, and presently, when she asked him, he told her something of the child on whom he had been operating.

'You'll go and see her again?'

'Yes. Would you like to come to the hospital with me?'

'Oh, yes, please.' She added hastily, 'I won't get in your way.'

'Everyone there wants to meet you...'

After that the days sped by, gradually forming a pattern which Margo could see was to be her life in the future. Pleasant hours with Gijs—walking, sitting by the fire talking and reading, learning to play pool in the billiard room at the back of the house—but also long hours spent on her own while he worked in his study and twice drove to Amsterdam where he spent most of the day.

Certainly he had taken her to the hospital at Utrecht, but as soon as they'd arrived he'd handed her over to an elderly *zuster*, who'd trotted round introducing her to the nurses on the wards. All the same, she'd gone back home with him feeling that she was sharing a very small piece of his working life.

She wasn't lonely, though. She spent time each morning with Kieke, and Wim helped out with the language—after a few days she began to pick out a word here and there, and even tried a word or two of Dutch herself.

She went down to the village too, and wandered round the church, examining the massive tombstones marking countless van Kessels. She met the *dominee* there, and he took her back to his house to drink coffee with his wife.

On Sundays she and Gijs went to church, and sat in the front pew, its little gate shutting them off from the rest of the congregation. The sermons were long and stern, and to her surprise, Gijs always took her hand in his and held it for the whole of the oration.

Perhaps, she thought hopefully, he's falling in love with me. But nothing in his behaviour suggested that.

Although there were no more trips to Utrecht, their days were filled. Friends called—so many people knew Gijs and were anxious to meet his bride—and they walked a great deal with the delighted Punch, and in the evenings they sat by the fire.

Gijs seemed content, Margo thought, although she suspected that he sometimes longed to go to his study and work or read. She had suggested it tentatively once or twice, but he had assured her that he had no wish to do so.

'I'm on holiday,' he had observed. 'Time enough for that when we're back in London.'

Leaving Arntzstein was a wrench; she had had no idea until the moment they left that she would mind going so much. The sight of Punch mournfully moaning quietly to himself as they got into the car made her tearful. They had driven some miles in silence before she could trust herself to speak.

'Don't you miss Punch?'

'Abominably. We must sneak over for a weekend as soon as I can manage it.'

'Oh, good. I shall miss him too—and your home...'

'Our home,' he corrected her quietly. 'I'm so glad you enjoyed our stay.'

'Oh, I did. I think I'd like to live there always...'

'Well, that is possible. I could go to and fro quite easily.'

She felt shocked. 'But you've bought that lovely little house in London.'

'We need a place there while I still work in England, but once it is furnished and we have settled in there is no reason why you shouldn't stay at Arntzstein for as long as you wish.'

'You'd be in London, though.'

'For some of the time, yes.'

'That wouldn't do at all,' said Margo roundly. 'I'm your wife.'

They talked about other things then, but at the back of her mind was the thought that Gijs would be quite willing to let her do as she wished. If he loved me, she thought miserably, he wouldn't even suggest it.

Once back in London they went straight to the house Gijs had rented. As he stopped the car Margo said suddenly, 'All the lights are on. There's someone there, Gijs.'

He said casually, 'My old nanny has a younger sister. I asked her to come as housekeeper.'

Margo turned to look at him. 'You think of everything, Gijs. You seem to have the gift of making things happen.'

'You think so? Everyone can make mistakes and I am no exception.'

CHAPTER EIGHT

MARGO didn't say anything as she got out of the car. What had Gijs meant. Had he been admitting that he had made a mistake in marrying her? Had it been just a random remark which meant nothing much? She was tempted to ask him, but now hardly seemed the right moment.

The door opened as they reached it and a stout elderly woman stood beaming a welcome.

'Master Gijs, welcome—and you, madam. There's the kettle boiling, for I've no doubt you'll be wanting a good cup of tea…'

The professor bent to kiss her plump cheek. 'Mattie, you've settled in? Did Nanny come to London with you?' He turned to Margo. 'Mattie is a very old friend,' he told her. 'When I was a small boy she used to come and visit Nanny and bring me bull's eyes.'

Mattie chuckled richly. 'Go on with you, Master Gijs. Fancy you remembering that. No, she didn't come with me.

'If you would like to come with me, madam, I'll take you upstairs.' As they went up together she said cheerfully, 'I dare say Mister Gijs forgot to tell you that I'd be here? I hope you won't take it in bad part, madam. He's asked me to housekeep for you, but it's for you to decide.'

They had reached the bedroom, which was softly lit with flowers in a vase and the curtains drawn against the dusk.

'I can't think of anything nicer than to have you for

a housekeeper, Mattie. I hope you'll stay with us always. I don't know London at all well and everything's a bit strange.' Margo smiled cheerfully at the elderly face, liking it already. 'Must you call me madam? Isn't there something else…?'

'Well, I could call you ma'am if you'd prefer.'

'Yes, please. This room looks lovely, and so welcoming. You must have worked hard.'

'It's an easy house. Mister Gijs said you had bought a mews cottage…'

'Yes, but it has to be furnished before we can move into it. It's bigger than this one—the rooms are larger. It's in a mews near the professor's consulting rooms. We shall be busy, you and I, Mattie.'

'It'll be a pleasure, ma'am.' Mattie bustled to the door. 'I'll get the tea—you'll be wanting a cup.'

Left to herself, Margo took a look round. Mattie had taken great pains to make the room look welcoming. There were magazines on the bedside table, and the long cupboard along one wall and the drawers in the chest smelled of lavender. She went through the half-open door into the bathroom beyond, and found that it had everything that she could possibly want.

She tidied herself and went downstairs to join Gijs in the sitting room. At the back of her mind was a feeling of resentment that he had installed Mattie without saying a word to her—on the other hand he might have done that to make her sudden plunge into married life easier. He would have overlooked the fact that it was a small house, which Margo could easily have run without any help. She went slowly into the sitting room and found him at a desk under the window, writing.

He pulled a chair forward for her by the fire and sat down opposite her.

'I must be at the hospital by eight o'clock tomorrow

morning and I shall be there all day. I'm sorry that I have to leave you alone, but I'll be free on Sunday. I thought we might go and see Aunt Florence, and when we come back we could go to the house and make a few decisions about furnishing it. The pieces you chose at Arntzstein will be sent over as soon as the floors and windows are ready. If we can decide something on Sunday, perhaps you would look around for carpets and curtains? We can collect the rest of the furniture at our leisure—there's a good place at Stow-on-the-Wold and another at Bath. It will be nice to have your own home.'

She had been steeling herself to the idea of being lonely until such time as she had found her way around and made a few friends, but obviously there wasn't going to be much time for loneliness. She said now, 'Well, will you tell me how much I can spend?'

'Of course. As soon as I have time we will go and arrange a bank account for you—for your own personal use. The bills for the house will, of course, be sent to me.'

She thanked him as Mattie came in with the tea, and he talked of something else then.

Later, after they had dined, he suggested that she should phone Aunt Florence.

Aunt Flo sounded brisk. 'Well, so you're back. What did you think of Holland?'

'I liked it very much,' said Margo. 'May we come and see you on Sunday? Gijs will be free. We plan to go and look at the house he's bought and decide about furnishing it, but if we might just call in...?'

'Come for tea—five o'clock. That gives you the whole day at the house. I'm going out to supper, but I dare say you'd like to be back for an evening at home together anyway.'

How cosy that sounds, thought Margo. But it

wouldn't be like that—they would dine and have their coffee and presently he would go to his study and she would read until she could go to bed. She frowned at her thoughts. She had no reason to complain; Gijs had his work and she had a lovely little home here and a magnificent one in Holland. She still had to find her feet...

She was secretly delighted when he stayed with her, talking about Arntzstein, discussing the house they would live in once they had furnished it to their liking; they would go over to Holland again in about six weeks' time, he told her. 'For about three weeks,' he said. 'But part of the time I shall be away from home. I'm sure you'll find plenty to do and you will have Beatrice to visit.'

'I'm quite sure that I shall be happy, Gijs. Shall we have the house here ready by then?'

'I don't see why not. Once we have decided what we need it is only a matter of buying exactly what we want.'

Margo, rather overawed at the idea of shopping on such a vast scale, agreed.

Gijs had been gone for an hour by the time she went down to breakfast in the morning. She had assured him that she didn't mind getting up early and having the meal with him, but had realised as she'd said it that he had no wish for her company. She had crept to the window and watched him drive away, hoping that he would look up, but he hadn't.

He was tired when he got home just before dinner that evening.

'I'll be down in ten minutes,' he told her. 'Pour me a drink, will you?'

Presently, settled in his chair, the drink beside him, he asked her if she had had a pleasant day.

'Delightful,' said Margo. 'But what about you? Or don't you want to talk about it? If you do, I'd love to hear.'

He looked faintly surprised. 'Would you? I have always had the impression that people don't like to know what goes on in operating theatres.'

'Well, I'm the exception. I dare say I won't understand half of it, but I'm interested.' When he hesitated she asked, 'Were you in Theatre all day?'

'No, no. I had a clinic this morning—that lasted until almost noon—then I went to the ward and from there to Theatre.'

'Did you have lunch?'

He laughed then. 'You sound just like a wife. I had a sandwich and coffee in Sister's office.'

Margo suppressed an instant stab of jealousy. Probably the sister was young and pretty and very clever. 'Well, Mattie has cooked a marvellous meal. Was your nanny a good cook too?'

'She made excellent chips—we had them for a treat when we had been good—and toffee. We all made toffee on wet afternoons.'

'You were a happy little boy...'

She felt such a surge of love that she couldn't speak for a moment.

'Yes, indeed I was. And you, Margo? Were you a happy child?'

'Yes, I was happy too. You never lose it, do you? The memory of happiness?'

'No—and what a good thing that is.'

Mattie came then to tell them that dinner was on the table—a delicious meal of soup, beef *en croûte* and apple crumble with cream, helped along by

Chardonnay. Margo had chosen the meal carefully; Gijs was a very large man, and she thought it very likely that meals, if he ever got to them, might not be eaten at the right times—and even then they might consist of sandwiches.

They talked about nothing much as they ate, comfortable with each other's company, and when Mattie brought them their coffee at the table Gijs observed, 'You haven't lost your touch, Mattie. Dinner was excellent.'

Mattie smiled widely. 'Well, now, Mr Gijs, I've kept my hand in, as it were, but the apple crumble Mrs van Kessel made—as good as ever I could myself!'

'How fortunate I am,' murmured the professor, 'with two good cooks to look after me. I must congratulate you both!'

The next morning Margo went to their mews cottage armed with a notebook, pen and tape measure. A practical girl, she drew a careful plan of the little place, putting in measurements, inspecting the rooms carefully and imagining them furnished.

The pieces from Arntzstein would fit in beautifully, though the furniture they bought would have to be of the same period. The floors were wooden, so they would have rugs downstairs and fitted carpets in the bedrooms. The kitchen had its original stone floor and would need matting in front of the Aga. The room leading from it would be Mattie's—another fitted carpet, Margo decided, and warm curtains at the window. And, since Mattie was going to live in it, she should be allowed to furnish it as she liked.

Margo went back for lunch then, and spent a delightful but tiring afternoon collecting samples of material for curtains, deciding on the best shop at which to get the carpets and browsing through Harrods' kitchen departments.

Gijs came home soon after she had had tea, but when she got up to get him a fresh pot he declined.

'I had a cup in Sister's office. What have you done with yourself today?'

She told him, showing him her carefully drawn plan and then the samples of material and the colour charts.

'If you aren't too tired would you tell me the kind of curtains you would like and the colours? I won't bother you again unless you want to be.' She hesitated. 'I don't expect you would have the time to come to the shop and choose with me?'

'The day after tomorrow. I'll come home for lunch and we'll go together. I'll have to go back to the hospital afterwards, and then on to my consulting rooms, but I can be free until four o'clock.'

How easy it was to shop, reflected Margo, sitting beside Gijs trying to decide exactly which shade of mulberry-red was right for the sitting-room curtains, when there was no need to look at the price ticket. What a good thing it was, too, that they had similar tastes when it came to carpets and curtains.

Chintz curtains in the bedrooms and mushroom fitted carpets, and no stair carpet, they agreed, since the small staircase was oak, with the patina of age. As for rugs and carpets downstairs, they would hunt for them in the Cotswolds, taking their time.

He drove her back on his way to the hospital and she spent a delightful half-hour with Mattie discussing Mattie's wishes for her own room before going to her room and changing into one of her pretty dresses. Probably Gijs wouldn't notice it, but she intended to leave no stone unturned.

She need not have bothered. He came home just after ten o'clock that evening, and, since the dinner Mattie had so lovingly prepared was ruined, Margo cooked him bacon and eggs and mushrooms and fried bread, and without asking poured him a glass of Guinness.

He came into the kitchen while she was cooking and sat himself down at the table. 'I didn't expect this,' he told her.

Margo prodded the bacon. 'Well, from now on you can. Don't forget that I was brought up in a household where the master of the house came and went at all hours of the day and night. Father—' she gulped in sudden sorrow '—was at everyone's beck and call. Just as I think you are.'

He said mildly, 'Neither your father nor I would wish for anything different.'

She nodded. 'So it's a good thing that you married me, isn't it?'

She was dishing up and didn't see his look. 'A very good thing,' he observed.

She sat opposite him while he ate and soon after poured coffee for them both, and in a little while he began to tell her of his afternoon's work. There had been complications at the hospital and the patients he had seen at his rooms had taken up more time than he had expected. Small children suffering from unpronounceable illnesses which she couldn't even guess at. She would have to get a medical dictionary, she reflected. She listened intelligently and went to bed presently, glowing with the thought that he had enjoyed talking to her.

On Sunday, when they went to the cottage, she was astonished to see that the bedroom carpets had already been fitted.

'But it's only been days...'

'I did mention that we wanted to move into the place as quickly as possible.' Gijs had wandered out into the tiny garden behind the cottage. 'The pieces from Arntzstein should be here this week. I should be free next Saturday—we might look for carpets. Persian in the sitting room, don't you think?'

They went home presently, and Margo cooked lunch as Mattie had her day off and had gone to visit a niece on the other side of London.

Aunt Florence was pleased to see them, and even more pleased were Caesar and Plato.

'Shall we take them back with us?' asked Margo.

'If you must. But wouldn't it be sensible to wait until you move into your own home?' Aunt Flo said matter-of-factly. 'Another week or two won't make much difference.'

So they went back to London without the animals, and, seeing Margo's downcast face, the professor said, 'We should be able to move in two weeks' time. Once we have the place furnished we can take our time with making it home.'

A very reassuring remark, Margo considered.

An accurate one, too, as it turned out. Standing in the centre of the cottage's kitchen, Margo revolved slowly, admiring the rows of new saucepans, the china on the wooden dresser they had found in a Cotswold town and the solid wooden table with the Windsor chairs at each end of it. There was still a good deal to do, she conceded, but the splendid Persian rug in the sitting room was exactly right with the Dutch marquetry cabinet and sofa table which had been brought over from Holland and the two sofas on each side of the fireplace were lovely.

The bedrooms were almost complete. The four-poster in her room was nicely offset by the applewood dressing table and bedside tables. They had found a chaise longue, too, for the foot of the bed, and two George IV bergères, whose faded tapestry upholstery blended nicely with the curtains. Downstairs in the hall was a long-case clock, walnut and marquetry, which they had come across quite by chance and for which Gijs had paid what Margo considered to be a small fortune.

There *was* still a lot to be done; the third bedroom was by no means complete and she was looking forward to a morning in Harrods choosing towels to match the bathrooms. But Mattie's room was finished, and as comfortable as it was possible to make it. She wandered upstairs and looked in Gijs's room. A picture or two would make it look cosier. She went over to the chest of drawers and picked up his hairbrushes, and then the little leather box where he kept his cuff-links. After a few moments she put them down gently and went out of the room, closing the door behind her.

She mustn't allow herself to get downhearted, even though Gijs seemed no nearer to falling in love with her. They had settled down to an easygoing comradeship, and she was sure that he enjoyed her company. All the same there was an invisible wall between them; she was being held, metaphorically speaking, at arm's length. He had told her that they could get to know each other once they were married and she had been content with that, but in two weeks' time they would go to Holland again, and they were no closer now than they had been when they had married.

'I mustn't worry about it,' said Margo aloud, and went back to the kitchen to see how Caesar and Plato had settled in.

That evening the professor's youngest sister phoned.

She was coming over to London to do some shopping and wanted to stay for a day or two.

'Can you manage, Margo?' asked Gijs. 'It's short notice…'

His youngest sister, Corinne, was his favourite. 'Of course,' said Margo happily; it would mean dashing out in the morning and buying one or two things, but Corinne wasn't coming for a couple of days yet. A small easy chair, thought Margo, and bedspreads for the beds, and that lovely flower painting I saw in that art gallery. 'It will be lovely to have her. Will she be on her own?'

'Yes, Julius is going to Sweden on business for a week.'

They had been married for two years, Margo remembered, and she wondered why Corinne didn't want to go to Sweden with him. A pity she didn't know Gijs well enough to ask him…

The room looked delightful when it was ready, with flowers in a little porcelain vase, a pile of fluffy towels in the bathroom and the bedspreads of pastel patchwork. Margo laid a small pile of magazines on one of the bedside tables, made sure that the water carafe was full and went downstairs to wait for her guest.

Corinne was laughing and talking to Gijs, who had been to fetch her from Heathrow, as they entered the cottage. She was a very pretty young woman and beautifully dressed, and she embraced Margo with warmth.

'What a dear you are to let me come and stay with you so soon after you're married. I promise I will not play gooseberry.' She trilled with laughter. 'I shall go shopping, and I do hope that you will come with me, but I promise I will not be a nuisance.'

'It's lovely to have you,' said Margo, and meant it.

'I love shopping, and Gijs and I are very pleased to see you.'

'I look forward to going to the theatre—it is a play I long to see—and the party will be such fun...'

Margo wiped the astonishment off her face and planted a smile there. Theatre? Party? It was the first she had heard of either. 'Come up to your room,' she invited. 'Tea will be in ten minutes or so.'

She took care not to look at Gijs, and led the way upstairs, made sure that Corinne had everything she needed then went back to the drawing room.

The professor was sitting in an armchair with Plato pressed up against his knees and Caesar perched on its arm.

'Don't get up,' said Margo in a voice to freeze him solid, and bent to give the fire an unnecessary poke.

'It was to be a surprise,' said the professor mildly. 'The theatre. My fault; I should have warned Corinne not to mention it. As for the party, that is something I had hoped to discuss with you this evening, but perhaps I should wait until you have gone off the boil!'

He gave her a friendly smile, having cut the ground neatly from under her.

'I am not—' began Margo, and then added, 'Oh, why are you always right?' She caught his eye and burst out laughing. 'You are sometimes a very tiresome man!' She added swiftly, 'And don't say that I am tiresome too, because I know that already.'

'Never tiresome, Margo. Indeed, since we married—' He broke off as the door opened and Corinne came in, followed by Mattie with the teatray. Margo wondered what he had been going to say as she handed out cups and offered toasted teacakes.

Later that evening, when Corinne had gone to bed,

he had the chance to tell her, but he didn't, merely brought up the subject of the party again.

'Dinner?' he wanted to know. 'Eight or ten of us? It's time you met some of my colleagues and their wives, and for Corinne we'll ask a couple of younger, unattached men. Will you agree to that? And, to make things easy, why don't you both come with me to the hospital governers' tea party on Saturday? It's hardly an exciting occasion, but I can introduce you to everyone and break the ice for you.'

Margo agreed; she suspected that if she hadn't he would still have got his own way. 'And the theatre?' she wanted to know.

'Tomorrow evening—can we dine early?'

She agreed readily, with the unhappy thought that he was exerting himself to amuse his sister but had failed to do the same for her. Time for another visit to the hairdresser and a prowl round the cosmetic counters, she decided. Perhaps a new dress? Supposing she dyed her hair? She had long, silky hair, but mouse-brown had never been in fashion. Highlights, perhaps? A hint of gold or even auburn…?

'What are you plotting?' Gijs said suddenly.

'I was deciding what to do about my hair. I think perhaps I'll have it cut very short and then high-lighted…'

'No,' said the professor, in such a forceful voice that she looked at him, surprised. 'I like your hair as it is; it suits your face.'

'Well, that's the whole point. If I had something dramatic done to my hair it might improve my looks.'

'Your looks are very nice as they are. I would much prefer you to leave your hair as it is.'

'Very well,' said Margo, reflecting that he probably found that her unassuming appearance didn't distract him from his work. She remembered the rather striking dress she had seen in Harrods' window; it would do nicely for the dinner party, and even if he didn't notice it the guests might...

Corinne was the ideal guest, knowing just when to disappear for an hour or so, and a delightful companion for Margo. They shopped the very next day, and while Corinne was trying on evening gowns Margo slipped away to look at the dress she had decided to buy herself. When she tried it on she could see that it wasn't for her—the colour was too vivid, the skirt was shorter than short and her sensible mind queried the sense of paying a great deal of money for a few yards of material, however costly that material was. Instead she chose something quite different—pink patterned chiffon over a silk slip, with an ankle-length skirt, long, tight sleeves and a modest neckline. She thought it likely that Gijs wouldn't notice it.

The visit to the theatre was a great success. Gijs had tickets for *Sunset Boulevard* and Margo sat entranced until the final curtain. She had loved every minute of it, and not only the performance but also the theatre, with its bright lights, and the audience, the music and the volume of voices during the interval. She sat like a mouse, noticing nothing else, and the professor, watching her rapt face, smiled to himself. It was rather like taking his nieces to the circus for the first time...

He took them to the Savoy for a late supper after the show, and Corinne's happy chatter made it unnecessary to do more than reply briefly from time to time.

On Saturday afternoon they went to the hospital governors' tea party and Margo was introduced to Gijs's colleagues and their wives, some of whom would be coming to the dinner party. They were friendly peo-

ple, bent on making her feel at home, and presently Gijs
went to speak to one of the governors, leaving her with
a group of the wives.

'We were so delighted when we heard that Gijs was
to marry,' said one lady, slightly older than the rest of
them. 'A consultant, especially a paediatrician, needs a
wife.' She beamed kindly at Margo. 'And I am sure
that you are exactly right for him—a vicar's daughter,
I believe?'

Margo said that yes, she was, and that she hoped she
would be a help to Gijs—a remark which earned her
the approbation of her listeners.

Gijs was still at the other end of the room, but she
could see Corinne talking animatedly to a youngish
man with dark good looks. They were getting on very
well together—perhaps they had met somewhere else.
Margo, mindful of good manners, bent her full attention
to a girl with a lisp, married to the hospital secretary,
who wanted to know what she had thought of Holland.

The intervening days before the dinner party were
taken up with more shopping on Corinne's part. 'I'm
going out on my own,' she told Margo gaily. 'You must
have heaps of things that you want to do and I know
my own way round. I'll stop out for lunch...'

Which suited Margo very well, for she wanted the
dinner party to be a success and she needed time to
have everything just so. She and Mattie had already put
their heads together and thought up a menu, and while
Mattie saw to the food she busied herself with the table
and the seating arrangements. Everyone who had been
asked had accepted.

When she told Gijs he said casually, 'Well, I expected them to—they are all dying of curiosity. They
met you at the hospital the other afternoon; now they
want to see us in our new home.' He looked up from

the papers he was studying. 'The wine will be delivered tomorrow. Leave it in the hall, and I'll take it down to the cellar when I get home.' After a few minutes he put down the papers.

'Where is Corinne?'

'Shopping again. She needs to buy so much, and she wanted to go on her own.'

Gijs smiled. 'She'll make Julius bankrupt.'

A joke, of course. All the same, Corinne *had* been buying a great many things, and once or twice, when Margo had asked her if her purchases were being delivered since she had come home empty-handed, she had told her light-heartedly that she had arranged to have them sent over to Holland.

'Heaven knows, I've enough luggage as it is,' she'd laughed.

It was quite late on the evening before the party when the senior consultant surgeon's wife phoned Margo. Could she possibly bring another guest? she wanted to know. 'This is unpardonable of me, my dear, but he is leaving England in a day or so and I hate to leave him on his own.' She added, 'Actually he is my husband's nephew.'

'Of course he must come,' said Margo, rearranging the table in her mind's eye. 'We shall be delighted to meet him.'

She said goodbye and rang off, and since Corinne was in her room and Gijs had been called back to the hospital to give his opinion on a small child who had fallen from a window in a block of flats she went to the kitchen to tell Mattie.

'I hope the professor won't mind,' she confided uneasily, 'although it will be nice for Corinne to meet a new face. There's plenty of food?'

'More than enough, ma'am. Can I get you anything before I go to bed?'

'No, thank you, Mattie; I dare say the professor will be very late back. There's coffee keeping warm for him, isn't there? I think I'll go to bed in a little while. I'll stay up a bit, just in case he doesn't stay.'

She said goodnight, made sure that Caesar and Plato were comfortable in their baskets, and went back to the drawing room. When the clock struck midnight she put the guard in front of the fire, made sure that the doors and windows were secure and took herself off to bed.

There was no light under Corinne's door. She would be tired after her long day—indeed, she seemed over-tired, reflected Margo, her eyes too bright and always talking non-stop. I shall miss her when she goes home, thought Margo, lying in bed wondering what Gijs was doing.

He was just starting on an operation to try and save the life of the small girl on the operating table, and he wouldn't be home for hours...

He was leaving the house as Margo went down to breakfast the next morning. He wished her good morning and she saw how tired he was.

'Have you had any sleep at all?'

'An hour or so.' He smiled. 'I'll catch up on sleep later. I'll see if I can be home in good time this evening.'

He was already at the door; it wasn't the moment to tell him about the extra guest. She told him to be careful in a motherly voice and watched him drive away.

'He works too hard,' she told Plato, and went to eat her breakfast. Corinne would be down presently, she supposed.

She appeared five minutes later, bubbling over with

chatter, talking about going back home, the clothes she had bought and the people she had met.

'It's been heavenly, so exciting…'

'Exciting? Well, I don't know about that,' observed Margo in her sensible way. 'We haven't done much to entertain you, though I dare say you've enjoyed all that shopping.'

Corinne giggled. 'Oh, the shopping—indeed I have!'

Margo, in the pink dress, was alone in the drawing room when Gijs came home. Their guests were due in half an hour, and after greeting her hurriedly he started for the stairs.

'Gijs.' She hurried to the door. 'There hasn't been a chance to tell you but Lady Colbert phoned late yesterday evening and asked if she might bring her husband's nephew—he's staying with them. It has made it rather awkward at the table, but I couldn't refuse.'

She had expected him to be annoyed; she hadn't expected the anger in his face. 'Jerome Colbert? Since he is to be our guest I can do nothing about it, but I must ask you and Corinne to have nothing more to do with him than common courtesy dictates.'

'Why?'

'I haven't time to explain now. Please accept my advice and do as I ask.'

'Am I to tell Corinne?'

He was going up the stairs. 'Yes—and I must add that Julius is of the same opinion as I am.'

Margo went back to the drawing room, rather shaken by Gijs's anger, and wondering how to be courteous to someone you had been asked to shun. She looked up as Corinne, a vision in a red silk sheath, came in.

Margo glanced at the clock; there were barely ten

minutes left in which to explain. 'Listen,' she said urgently. 'That nephew of Lady Colbert's—Gijs says...'

She relayed his words and was surprised to see Corinne's look of glee.

'Don't tell, but I've been seeing him every day—just for fun, you know. He's so amusing. I told him about this evening and he persuaded his aunt.' She giggled as she sat down.

'But Corinne, Gijs said— What would he say if he knew?'

'Promise you won't tell.' Corinne suddenly looked anxious. 'You must promise, Margo. Gijs'll be so angry with me, and he'll tell Julius or make *me* tell him and Julius will be furious. He's cross with me as it is.' She shrugged. 'You know how it is—we quarrelled and he went off to Sweden on his own. I was only having some fun—nothing serious!' She got up and went to sit by Margo and caught her hand in hers. 'Margo, promise—please? Julius will never forgive me, and I know he's a bit dull, but I do love him.'

'I promise,' said Margo, and turned a serene face to Gijs as he came into the room.

The guests arrived and Margo, standing beside Gijs, welcoming them, did her best to dismiss Corinne's problems from her mind. But she was reminded of them when the Colberts arrived.

Sir Anthony was elderly, within a few years of retirement, and a distinguished and respected surgeon and firm friend of Gijs. His wife was charming but inclined to dominate the wives in her circle. Luckily for Margo, she had taken a liking to her, and greeted her warmly, admiring her dress and the pleasant little house.

'Here is my nephew whom you so kindly invited.' She introduced the man Margo had seen talking to Corinne at the tea party and she shook hands, murmuring a welcome, aware that Gijs, standing beside her, nodded at him but didn't shake hands and his greeting was coolly polite.

With everyone in the drawing room having drinks, Margo circulated, moving from one group to the next, well versed in the hostess's job and trying to keep an eye on Corinne. It was a relief to see that she was at the other end of the room to Jerome.

They were seated at opposite ends of the table too, and as far as she could see they had had no chance to speak to each other apart from a brief greeting. So far so good, thought Margo, counting her chickens before they were hatched.

It was after dinner, while they were drinking their coffee, that Gijs and Sir Anthony excused themselves to go to the study and look at a paper the elder man wished to see. A minute or two later Margo, caught up in a lengthy conversation with several of the ladies, saw Corinne slip away, and a few minutes later Jerome left the room.

Short of getting up and leaving her guests in mid-sentence there was nothing Margo could do; all she could hope for was that Corinne and Jerome would return before Gijs. They did and she heaved a sigh of relief. It was short-lived, however, for Corinne caught her eye and gave her a look of panic, instantly hidden by a glittering smile as she joined them. As for Jerome, he was careful not to speak to Corinne again for the rest of the evening.

Presently their guests went home and Margo went to the kitchen to see if Mattie and her teenage nephew had coped and to thank them.

'A splendid dinner, Mattie,' she said, 'and thank you both.' She went to a drawer and took out some money and paid the youth. 'We're grateful that you could come and give a hand,' she told him. 'How will you get home?'

'Catch a bus,' he told her. 'And thanks for the money. I'll be off.'

'I'll be off to my bed, too,' said Mattie. 'A first-rate evening, ma'am. How about you having breakfast in bed in the morning?'

'Me? No, thank you, Mattie. I'm not tired and I like to have breakfast with the professor if he's home.'

She went back to the drawing room and Corinne said at once, 'It was a lovely evening, Margo—you were marvellous. Now I'm going to bed.'

She kissed them both and went upstairs.

'A very pleasant evening, Margo. You are a splendid hostess,' said Gijs. 'I was glad to see that both you and Corinne managed to keep away from young Colbert.'

'We did our best. Are you going to tell me about him?'

'Yes…' The phone rang and he picked it up and presently put it down again. 'I have to go. There's been a road accident—a baby and a toddler injured. Go to bed, Margo.'

She saw him out of the house with a quiet goodnight, turned out the lights and went upstairs to her room. She was sitting at her dressing table staring at her reflection when there was a tap on the door and Corinne came in.

'Where's Gijs?' she whispered. 'I must talk to you, Margo.'

'He's gone to the hospital. Can I help, Corinne?'

'I've been silly,' said Corinne, 'and I don't know what to do.'

'Tell me,' said Margo.

CHAPTER NINE

CORINNE settled herself on the side of the bed. 'It all started as fun. You see, I was cross with Julius; we quarrelled and he went off to Sweden on his own, and so I came here.

'And when Jerome got friendly I thought I would pay Julius back for being so tiresome. I didn't go shopping, you know; I met Jerome every day. I did tell you that this evening, didn't I? Only now I'm a little frightened.

'Jerome has become quite nasty—he wishes me to have an affair with him, and says if I won't he will tell Gijs, who I think will kill him if Julius doesn't kill him first. He insists that I meet him tomorrow afternoon but I do not dare. I will go back home on the first flight I can get in the morning.'

She turned a tearful gaze on Margo. 'Dear Margo, will you meet him for me and explain that I wasn't serious? Make him understand—you are always so serious; he will listen to you.'

'Supposing we go together?'

'That will not do at all, for now he frightens me. I want to go home to my Julius and in a little while I will tell him. He loves me very much so he will forgive me.' She added eagerly, 'No one needs to know that you have seen Jerome, and you have promised not to tell anyone. It can be our little secret.'

'Gijs asked me to have nothing to do with Jerome.'

'Darling Margo, he won't know, and besides, you're not meeting him because you want to, only to help me.'

Corinne began to weep in earnest. 'Whatever shall I do if he tells Julius? We love each other very much, you know. You must understand how I feel—supposing you were me and Gijs was Julius?'

She got up and flung her arms around Margo. 'You will help me, dear, kind Margo? Just this once?'

'Very well,' said Margo. 'Tell me where he will be and at what time.'

'At three o'clock. On the steps of the National Gallery. Now I will phone Heathrow and book a seat on a morning plane.'

'What will you tell Gijs?'

'I will tell him nothing. I will go when he has gone to the hospital and you can explain that Julius phoned and asked if I would go home—said that he was no longer angry.'

'That's not true.'

'It will be. When I am home I am certain that is what he will say. You do not like to tell a fib, I know, but this is such a little one and it hurts no one, Margo.'

Her next remark clinched the matter.

'I think that I am going to have a baby...'

Long after Corinne had booked her morning flight and gone to bed, Margo sat up in bed worrying, until her common sense told her that that would do no good at all. She had promised to help Corinne and that was that, however much she disliked the idea. Getting to sleep was a different matter, though. It was after two o'clock in the morning when she heard Gijs's quiet tread pass her door, and only then did she sleep.

When she went down to breakfast it was to find him gone. Which was a good thing, she reflected, for he was the one person she would have gone to for advice.

'Something I can't do,' she told Plato, who was gob-bling the toast she couldn't eat. 'So it's a good thing he isn't here.'

She wanted him there, though—his vast, calm, re-assuring person sitting opposite her, telling her what to do...

Corinne joined her presently, quite recovered from her frightened outburst about Jerome. She kissed Margo, informed her cheerfully that her bags were packed and asked if she could phone for a taxi to take her to Heathrow.

Margo saw her off during the morning. 'You will go and see Jerome?' asked Corinne anxiously. 'And you won't tell anyone?'

'No, I won't tell. I only hope I can make him un-derstand. He's bound to be angry.'

'Oh, dear—but only for a little while,' said Corinne airily, and smiled brilliantly. 'You have no idea how happy I am to have the whole silly business settled.'

To which Margo said nothing, choking back what her father would have described as her baser feelings.

It was a relief when, after a half-eaten lunch, she could get ready for her rendezvous. It was a cold day, and she buttoned herself into her cashmere coat, chose a felt hat which she hoped added dignity to her ap-pearance, told Mattie that she would be back for tea and set out.

She prudently stopped the taxi on the far side of Trafalgar Square and walked unhurriedly to the National Gallery, aware that if Jerome was already there he would be able to see her.

He was there, all right, halfway up the steps and looking in the opposite direction, so that he turned with surprise when she said quietly, 'Good afternoon, Jerome.'

'Mrs van Kessel—Margo. This is unexpected—I mean, I hardly expected to see you here...' He was flustered, and that gave her heart.

'Well, no, you expected Corinne, didn't you? I've come instead...'

'She's ill?'

'No, she has gone back to Holland. She asked me to come here and explain to you...'

When he would have spoken she said, 'No, let me finish. She asked me to tell you that she is sorry to have misled you—it was light-hearted fun on her part, a game until she returned home to her husband.'

'I don't believe you,' he blustered. 'She said—I was led to believe...'

'Never mind that now, and anyway you should have known better than to flirt with her.'

'Flirt!' His sneer was ugly. 'What do you know about flirting? I don't suppose any man has bothered to look at you more than once.'

'Probably not,' agreed Margo calmly. 'But rudeness won't help you, will it? Corinne intends to tell her husband how foolish she has been.' She added severely, 'It was very wrong of you to encourage her.'

He gobbled with rage. 'Really? And who are you to tell me what I may and may not do? Corinne egged me on.'

'Don't make matters worse with excuses. You should mend your ways.' She nodded a brisk goodbye. 'I don't expect to meet you again.'

She went back down the steps and hailed a taxi, feeling pleased with herself.

* * *

Fortunately for her peace of mind she was unaware that Gijs, caught up in a traffic jam in Trafalgar Square, was a surprised and angry witness to her meeting with Jerome. Glancing idly round, he had seen her at once. What was more, he could see that she and Jerome were apparently deep in an interesting talk, and when Jerome put his hands on Margo's shoulders he had difficulty in preventing himself from jumping out of his car and throttling the man. It was a pity he wasn't near enough to hear Margo's icy, 'Take your hands off me!'

The traffic untangled itself then, and he was forced to drive on. He was already late for his clinic for Down's Syndrome babies and toddlers, and somehow he managed to erase Margo from his mind so that by the time he reached the clinic he appeared his usual kindly self, listening patiently to anxious parents, examining the little ones gently, giving advice and offering hope.

When the last small patient had been borne away he had tea with Sister, giving no sign of haste, before getting into his car and driving back to his rooms to go over his appointments book with his secretary. Finally, he drove himself home.

Margo was in the drawing room with Caesar and Plato, and, despite the fact that she had told herself over and over again that she had no need to feel guilty for she had done nothing wrong, she heard Gijs's steps in the hall with a nasty sinking feeling.

He came quietly into the room, greeted her in his usual quiet voice and went over to the table by the window to pour their drinks.

Margo got to her feet, spilling an indignant Caesar

onto the floor. 'Have you had a good day?' she asked, and then, unable to put it off, began, 'Corinne...'

He turned to look at her. 'Yes?'

'She's gone home,' said Margo in a rush. 'Julius is back and—and wanted her to return as soon as possible. And as there was a seat on the late morning flight she took it. It was all a bit of a rush.' She stopped talking, aware that she was beginning to babble.

Gijs sat down. 'All rather sudden, wasn't it?'

'Well, yes, but I expect she wanted to see Julius again. She said she would phone you this evening and she was sorry not to see you to say goodbye.'

There was a silence then, fortunately broken by Mattie coming to tell them that dinner was ready, and Margo, feeling that she had crossed her bridge safely, allowed herself a certain amount of complacency.

A mistake. Drinking coffee in the drawing room after dinner, Gijs asked casually, 'And you, Margo—what have you done with yourself today?'

She spoke too quickly. 'Me? Oh, nothing much. I phoned Aunt Flo and did the flowers...'

'You didn't go out?'

He watched the colour creep into her face.

'Well, yes, I did. Just out, you know—nowhere special.'

Gijs reflected with bitter amusement that Margo, a vicar's daughter, was hopeless at being devious. He asked in a quiet voice which chilled her to the bone, 'And are the steps of the National Gallery not special?'

'The steps...?' She faltered, staring across at his impassive face, seeing the controlled anger in it.

'You were there, were you not?' His voice was silky. 'I was in a traffic jam and I saw you and Jerome together. Not a chance encounter, I imagine? There was a certain familiarity…you were absorbed in each other…'

When Margo said nothing, staring at him with eyes suddenly enormous in a white face, he added, 'I asked you to have nothing to do with him, Margo. Had you forgotten that? Or was the attraction so great? Will you tell me about it?'

She shook her head. 'I'd rather not.'

'I realise that perhaps you are bored with your life here, that it holds little excitement, and Jerome is young and good-looking and adept at charming women. I thought that you—' He stopped, and then continued levelly, 'Perhaps we can discuss the whole thing at our leisure some time. Unfortunately, I have a great deal of work for the next week and shall be seldom at home. Why not spend it with Aunt Florence?'

Margo swallowed tears. He was angry, but he didn't seem to care enough to ask her why she had gone to see Jerome; he had just taken it for granted that she had been bored. Not that she could have told him the truth, but he might have asked. He didn't care tuppence about her; she might just as well be with Aunt Flo.

'Very well, I'll go tomorrow.'

'Just tell me this, Margo. Did you go to see Jerome of your own free will? Had you arranged to meet him?'

She could only nod, looking no higher than his tie— which was a good thing; his face might have frightened her.

'I'll go to bed,' said Margo.

She didn't sleep, of course, but when she went down to breakfast the next morning she found Gijs already there. He wished her good morning exactly as usual, only as she sat down he asked her when she planned to go to Aunt Flo's.

'After lunch, I thought. There's a train…'

'I'll ring for a car and a man to drive you down. Will half past two suit you?'

She thanked him. He was making sure that she went, she thought miserably.

'Enjoy your visit,' he told her. 'I dare say that you have some plans. I hope you will behave with discretion. Aunt Florence is too nice to be upset.'

'Behave? Behave? Whatever do you mean?' Margo's normally mild nature flared into temper. 'How dare you talk to me like that? What in heaven's name have I got to be discreet about?'

She got up, quelling an urge to throw her coffee-cup at him. 'If that's the way you are going to talk, then I'm glad I don't have to see you for a week.' She added, quite reckless now, 'Perhaps it had better be for a month, or a year—or for ever…'

Gijs remained unmoved. 'That is entirely up to you, Margo.' He even smiled a little, although it wasn't a very nice smile. 'Sit down and finish your breakfast.'

'No, I won't,' said Margo, and flew out of the room and upstairs to her bedroom, where she had a thoroughly comforting weep before washing her face and going downstairs again—reluctantly, but there was nothing else to be done…

He had gone. Mattie, clearing the table, remarked cheerfully that the master was a one for work and no mistake. 'And you'll be off after lunch, ma'am? If you'd tell me what to cook for the professor… He said he'd be out all day but he will want a good meal in the evening. A week, he said. You'll miss each other, I'll be bound.'

She glanced at Margo's pale face and added sympathetically, 'It's hard when you can't be together when you're first wed.'

Margo remembered then that she hadn't phoned Aunt Flo. Supposing she was away or didn't want a guest? But when she rang it was to hear that Gijs had already phoned. He thinks of everything, thought Margo peevishly.

She didn't like leaving Caesar and Plato.

'Don't you worry, ma'am,' said Mattie. 'The master will take Plato out before he goes in the morning and when he gets home in the evening, and Caesar is happy enough in the garden. I'll take good care of them.'

Aunt Florence was pleased to see her. 'Need a change from London, do you?' she wanted to know. 'Gijs told me he was very busy—don't suppose you see much of each other.' She took a look at Margo's face. 'You look down in the dumps, child.' She sounded brisk. 'A good long walk in the fresh air will do you good. The Truemans have asked us to dinner tonight and the rector and his wife are coming to dinner tomorrow evening. Not exciting, but I dare say you will enjoy a change of scene.'

The week seemed never-ending, and although Margo dreaded seeing Gijs again she longed for him. Obedient to her aunt, she took long walks each morning, ate the nourishing food Phoebe cooked, and made conversation with various of Aunt Flo's friends who called. She described Arntzstein in minute detail to her, behaved just as she should at the Truemans', and made a reluctant fourth at Aunt Flo's bridge evening.

On her last evening she received a phone call from the driver who had brought her to Sunningfield. He would come for her at two o'clock on the following day, if that suited her— 'But Professor van Kessel says you are to do as you wish, madam.'

'I'll be ready at two o'clock,' said Margo. Gijs wanted her back; they would be sensible and talk quietly and she would explain that she didn't care a row of pins for Jerome, although how she was going to do that without giving away Corinne's part in the miserable business was a problem she had yet to solve.

Since it was a Saturday she was sure that he would be at home, but only Mattie was there, ready with tea and a warm welcome. Margo, with Plato and Caesar for company, nibbled sandwiches and pondered what she would say and presently went to her room and changed into a patterned silk dress in a pleasing shade of forest-green. She took pains with her hair and her make-up too, and went down again to sit in the drawing room and wait.

Gijs came home a scant half-hour before dinner. He came into the room unhurriedly, his hello pleasant, so that she took heart.

'It's nice to be home,' she told him. 'Have you been at the hospital?'

He sat down opposite her. 'No, I spent the afternoon with friends and stayed for drinks.' He pulled Plato's ears gently. 'You enjoyed your stay with Aunt Florence?'

She began to tell him about her week, only to realise halfway through that he wasn't listening. She stopped talking then, and presently they sat down to dinner. It was better then, for good manners forced him to make some sort of a reply to her efforts at conversation, and she felt more cheerful as they went back to the drawing room.

She had poured their coffee and was searching for something to talk about when he said casually, 'I am going over to Holland tomorrow. If you remember, I did intend going within the next week or so, but I find that I can leave here for the time being and there are several urgent cases in Utrecht I want to deal with.'

'Not me?' asked Margo, regardless of grammar.

'I think not. You must feel free to do as you wish, Margo.' He gave her a steady look. 'You still feel that you are unable to talk to me? Believe me, I will listen sympathetically. I am not so middle-aged that I cannot appreciate that one can fall in love whether one wishes to or not. We have been good friends—can you not confide in me?'

She shook her head, not looking at him; if she did she might forget her promise.

'I leave early in the morning. Draw on our account at the bank for any money you need. I have left our solicitor's phone number in case you need advice of any kind.'

She asked in a wispy voice, 'How long will you be away?'

'Difficult to say, but you can count on two weeks at least—possibly longer.'

There seemed to be nothing more to say, so she drank her coffee and said that she hoped he would have a safe journey. 'Please give my love to Punch. I—I rather think I'll go to bed; I'm tired.'

He opened the door for her, and as she passed him he kissed her hard. It was almost her undoing. Another moment and she would have told him everything, promise or no promise. Instead she flew upstairs to her room.

Sitting on the bed, she told herself that the kiss had

been his goodbye—not just for a few weeks but for ever.

She slept badly and got up early, hoping that she might see him before he left the house, but when she went downstairs Mattie was clearing away his breakfast things, pausing only to wish her good morning and suggest scrambled eggs.

'Feel a bit down, I dare say, ma'am, but he'll be back just as soon as he can. A good cup of coffee will make you feel more cheerful.'

Margo thanked the good soul, reflecting that it would take more than a cup of coffee to cheer her up; she would have to plan her days so that they were filled. Long walks in the park with Plato, visits to the picture galleries and the museums. The British Museum was in itself large enough to absorb at least two weeks, and perhaps by then Gijs would be home again.

She kept resolutely to her plans for the whole of that week—walking herself tired each morning, stuffing her head with useful information from a number of museums and picture galleries in the afternoon and working away at a tapestry cushion in the evening. There was no news of Gijs, and in the middle of the second week she allowed panic to take over.

He had left her; he was never going to see her again—never even write or telephone. Presently she pulled herself together; he wouldn't do any of those things. He might be angry and unforgiving but he was fair. Perhaps, she thought, he was waiting for her to make the first move. Perhaps he expected her to ask for a divorce—no, she corrected herself, an annulment.

She thought about this for some time, and then made up her mind as to what she should do.

* * *

Mattie wasn't at all surprised when she told her that she was going over to Holland.

'The professor wants you there, I dare say, ma'am. Can't get away, most likely.'

'I'll try and get a flight tomorrow, Mattie, and let you know how long I'm staying when I get there. Will you be all right with Caesar and Plato—would your nephew take Plato out each day if I leave some money for him?'

'He'll be glad to do that, ma'am. Saving up for one of those nasty motorbikes, he is.'

'Oh, good. I'll leave you plenty of money—did the professor say anything about your wages? I forgot to ask him.'

'Paid me before he went, ma'am.' She smiled cosily. 'Just you go to Holland. I'll keep an eye on things here until you're back.'

She had been lucky, thought Margo, looking down at the coastline of England as the plane gained height. There had been a seat available on a flight in the early afternoon. She had packed a small case, dressed herself in the blue cashmere dress and wrapped herself into her topcoat, and, mindful of first impressions, had perched a brown velvet hat with an upturned brim on her carefully arranged hair.

With the same object in view she had spent a long time before the looking glass doing things to her face, but somehow she hadn't looked right when she had finished, so she had taken all the make-up off again. Her face looked its best with cream, powder and lipstick and nothing else.

Schiphol was vast and busy. It took time to reach the street at last—or rather several streets, choked with buses and cars. She stood for a moment, getting her bearings, and presently saw an empty taxi.

At least she didn't have the worry of wondering whether she had enough money, she thought, getting in. She had plenty; Gijs had seen to that.

'I hope you speak English?' she said to the driver, and was relieved when he nodded.

'Enough, *mevrouw*.'

'Would you take me to a village called Arntzstein? It's a few miles from Utrecht.'

She had had time to look at a map before she left home; it was fifty or so kilometres from Sciphol.

Once they were clear of the airport and on the motorway, the driver drove fast. Margo was still rehearsing what she would say to Gijs when he turned off the highway and presently reached Arntzstein.

'It's through the village—you can see the gates at the end of that lane after the church.'

There were lights shining from the house. She got out, paid the driver, tipped him lavishly and climbed the steps to the door. She tried the handle but it was locked, so she pulled the old-fashioned bell. Funny to ring your own front doorbell, she reflected, and smiled at Wim when he opened the door.

It was nice to be welcomed so warmly. 'You have come to stay, *mevrouw*—what a pleasure for us all! Please to wait. I will fetch Kieke and she will take you to your room. We had it prepared; we had expected you...'

Kieke came, with Diny and Mien, to shake her hand and exclaim with delight at the sight of her.

'Such a surprise for the professor when he returns home,' said Kieke, going upstairs with Margo to make sure that everything was as it should be.

Margo agreed, quelling sudden panic.

When she went downstairs again, Wim was in the hall.

'Wim,' said Margo, 'please don't say a word to the professor when he comes in—I want to surprise him. When do you expect him?'

Wim beamed. 'How delighted he will be, mevrouw. He is expected sometime after six o'clock. If I bring tea now...'

'Yes, please. I'll have it in the small sitting room. I expect the professor will go straight to his study.'

'Always, *mevrouw*.' He was delighted at the idea of a conspiracy. 'You will remain there, *mevrouw*?'

'Yes, Wim. Where is Punch?'

'With the professor. He will also be delighted that you are here, *mevrouw*.'

She had her tea sitting by the cheerful fire in the cosy room and then, feeling nervous, got up and wandered around, looking at the photos in their silver frames and the family portraits hung on the walls.

The house was quiet so she heard Gijs and Punch come into the hall. She turned off the table-lamp, although the room was out of sight of the hall, and stood with a thumping heart, listening to distant voices. Not visitors, surely? She went to the door and opened it a crack and heard Gijs call to Punch as he crossed the hall and went into his study, shutting the door with a firm click.

Margo counted to ten to give him time to sit in his chair and to allow her heart to quieten down a bit. She wished now that she had never come, but this was something which couldn't be avoided. Moral courage, her father had once told her, was as important as the physical kind. She opened the door, crossed the hall and opened the study door.

Gijs looked up and got slowly to his feet, and Punch padded over to her, lifting his head to have his ears rubbed in Margo's special way.

'This is unexpected,' said the professor. 'Won't you sit down?'

When she had, he sat down again himself, watching her without speaking so that she made haste to break the silence.

'I thought we had better have a talk,' she began, and looked at him across the desk. He was tired, and there were lines she hadn't noticed before etched on his face, but he was impassive, waiting for her to go on.

'I don't know much about it,' said Margo, 'but I think we can be annulled. I mean, that's better than being divorced, isn't it? I expect you could arrange that? I've been thinking about it a great deal and I expect you have too...'

His brief grave nod did nothing to encourage her to have any hope. She went on doggedly, 'You see, you don't trust me, do you? And things will never be right between us, will they?'

He said evenly, 'If you wish for an annulment, Margo, it can be arranged.'

'That's what you want too. I've been a disappointment to you, haven't I?'

She paused, wishing with her whole heart that he would tell her that it didn't matter about Jerome, that they could start again, that everything would be all right...

'I want you to be happy, Margo,' was all that he said.

She could think of nothing more to say then; she had

said what she had come to say and it had broken her heart. She stood up.

'You will stay here as long as you wish,' said the professor, going to open the door for her. 'I hope Kieke has made you comfortable. If there is anything you need you have only to ask.'

His cold courtesy chilled her to the bone.

'Yes—yes, thank you. I'll go back to London to-morrow.'

'In that case let us say goodbye. I am going out immediately and shall not be returning until late tomorrow evening.'

She stared up into his face. 'Gijs...'

'No, let us say nothing more, my dear. You are unhappy and I love you too much to allow that.

'You love me? Oh, Gijs, what am I to do?' She was suddenly distraught.

He smiled. 'Why, surely that is obvious. I'm sure that young Colbert is waiting for you.'

He might be smiling, but he was in a cold rage, his eyes hard and stony. Unless she broke her promise to Corinne there was nothing more to be said, but a promise was a promise.

She went back to the little sitting room and sat there, icy cold despite the fire. Somehow she must put a brave face on things, make some excuse to Wim, get a seat on a plane and be well away before Gijs came back. He had made it clear that he didn't want to see her again.

She had no idea how long she had been sitting there when Wim came to tell her that dinner had been served. She went to the dining room and ate her solitary meal, agreeing with Wim that it was a great pity that the professor had been called away. 'I have to go back to

London tomorrow,' she told him. 'Will you see if you can get me a seat on an afternoon plane, Wim?'

Presently, in the kitchen, presiding over supper, Wim declared himself concerned. 'Something's not right,' he told Kieke. '*Mevrouw's* going back to London tomorrow almost as soon as she's got here and the professor went out of the house on his own. It's disturbing...'

There was no hurry in the morning—after all, Gijs wasn't coming back until the late evening. Margo went round the gardens exchanging talk with the gardener; neither of them could understand what the other was saying but that hardly mattered. She wanted to see everything before she left—the neat kitchen garden, the greenhouse, the swimming pool tucked away behind the shrubbery, the rose garden, bare now but surely a lovely sight in the summer. She went back indoors to be met with the news that her flight had been booked.

'I've got you a seat in the late afternoon, *mevrouw*,' said Wim. 'Five o'clock—if we leave here at three o'clock that should be time enough. No need for you to wait too long at Schiphol.'

She had lunch and then wandered round the house, going in and out of the rooms, looking at everything, picking up ornaments and putting them down again. Then she made her way to the attic. It was cold there, and a bit dusty, and quite a lot of the furniture had gone to the London house, but there was plenty left for her to look at: stacks of pictures against one wall, a loveseat upholstered in faded velvet, a magnificent doll's house and in one corner the cradle she had admired. All the van Kessels had been rocked in it, Gijs had said.

She sat down beside it, running a finger along its delicate woodwork, and started to cry.

The professor, with Punch beside him, had got into his car and driven himself to Friesland—a journey of just over a hundred miles.

He'd had time to think as he'd driven to the small farm he owned there, to be greeted with unsurprised pleasure by the old farmer and his wife who looked after it for him. They were accustomed to his erratic visits, if and when he could spare the time, and found it quite normal to prepare his room and give him supper. They had been equally unsurprised when he'd told them that he would leave early in the morning, since he had appointments at the hospital.

He'd eaten the simple meal they'd offered him and gone to his room with Punch at his heels, and presently he'd gone to bed to lie awake thinking of a future without Margo.

He was too old, he'd thought wearily, and Jerome Colbert was a past master at charming women. Margo wasn't his usual type of woman, though—perhaps he really had reformed and loved her...

He'd driven back to Utrecht in the early morning, glad of Punch's warm body beside him. When he had finished at the hospital he would go home and talk to Margo again...

He had dealt with his small patients and was having his coffee in Sister's office when he was requested to go to his own office, where he had a visitor.

It wasn't Margo; it was Corinne. He schooled his features into a welcoming smile and asked her what he could do for her. 'You look worried,' he added. 'Have you come out without your purse?'

She shook her head. 'Gijs, Julius said that I must come and tell you. You'll be angry with me.' She gave him a beseeching look. 'It was all just for fun, you see. Only then he got nasty…'

Gijs sat down at his desk. 'Go on.'

'Jerome—you know, Jerome Colbert—you told Margo we weren't to have anything to do with him. Well, he seemed such fun…'

It all came tumbling out then, until she said finally, 'So, you see, it wasn't anything to do with Margo, but I made her promise not to tell, and Julius says that it was wrong of me to ask her because she might want to tell you. So I thought that when you got back to London you could tell her first. She doesn't like him, you know, but she went to see him instead of me because she knew that Julius loved me and that he might be very angry. She knows that I love Julius too, and I'm going to have a baby.' She burst into tears and Gijs got up and took her in his arms.

'What splendid news, my dear, and don't worry about Margo; she's at Arntzstein.' He smiled thinly. 'But don't, I beg of you, *liefje*, ask her to make any more promises. Remember that she was brought up to keep them. At all costs.'

Corinne mopped her eyes, declared him to be the best brother any girl could wish for and went away, her spirits quite restored. As for the professor, he sat down at his desk and picked up the phone, rearranging his day so that he could go home at once. It was still early afternoon and Margo might still be there…

The house was quiet as he went in, but Wim came to him in the hall.

'*Mevrouw* is still here?' asked Gijs.

Wim nodded. 'I shall be driving her to Schiphol at four o'clock, Professor.'

'No, you won't,' said Gijs. 'Where is she, Wim?'

'I am not sure, *mijnheer*. She went upstairs some time ago—perhaps she is in her room?'

The professor, with Punch at his heels, went up the staircase and knocked on Margo's door. When there was no answer he went in. There was no one there, only her overnight bag standing ready packed.

He looked in the other rooms on that landing, and was standing at the head of the staircase deciding where to look next when he heard a faint sound. Somewhere on the floor above? He went up a second flight of stairs, found no one in any of the rooms, and then opened a door in the landing wall. The sound was louder now, and he went up the narrow, steep stairs two at a time and opened the attic door.

Margo was still by the cradle; the first few tears had turned into a torrent. She sniffed and sobbed and snuffled, oblivious of time or place, hopelessly unhappy.

The professor stood in the doorway, looking at her sitting there, clinging to the cradle, and when he made a slight movement and she looked up he thought she had never looked so beautiful, her white face streaked by grubby tears, her eyelids puffy, her hair in a fine tangle.

He was across the floor and she was in his arms before she had time to do more than gasp.

'Don't say a word, my darling. Corinne came to see me. Dear heart, could you not have told me? A promise is a promise, but surely there should be no secrets between man and wife?'

Margo gulped. 'Oh, Gijs, I wish I'd thought of that.'

Her voice was thick with tears. 'I nearly did tell you when you said you loved me…'

'Forgive me, Margo. I have loved you for so long, have waited patiently for you to love me, and I thought that I had lost you.'

'Lost me? But I love you, Gijs. I didn't know until we were getting married.' She peered up into his face and smiled at what she saw there. 'Oh, Gijs, don't leave me ever again.'

He kissed her then, which was actually a much more satisfactory answer than any words.

Punch's polite yawn caused them to look round. He was sitting by the cradle, patiently waiting, so they walked to the door, turning to have a last look.

'The cradle will need a good polish…' said Margo, standing on tip-toe to reach her husband's cheek.

For a limited time, Harlequin and Silhouette have an offer you just can't refuse.

In November and December 1998:

BUY **ANY** TWO HARLEQUIN
OR SILHOUETTE BOOKS and
SAVE $10.00
off future purchases

OR BUY ANY THREE HARLEQUIN OR SILHOUETTE BOOKS
AND **SAVE $20.00** OFF FUTURE PURCHASES!

(each coupon is good for $1.00 off the purchase of two
Harlequin or Silhouette books)

JUST BUY 2 HARLEQUIN OR SILHOUETTE BOOKS, SEND US YOUR
NAME, ADDRESS AND 2 PROOFS OF PURCHASE (CASH REGISTER
RECEIPTS) AND HARLEQUIN WILL SEND YOU A COUPON BOOKLET
WORTH $10.00 OFF FUTURE PURCHASES OF HARLEQUIN OR
SILHOUETTE BOOKS IN 1999. SEND US 3 PROOFS OF PURCHASE AND
WE WILL SEND YOU 2 COUPON BOOKLETS WITH A TOTAL SAVING OF
$20.00. (ALLOW 4-6 WEEKS DELIVERY) OFFER EXPIRES
DECEMBER 31, 1998.

I accept your offer! Please send me a coupon booklet(s), to:

NAME: _____

ADDRESS: _____

CITY: _____ STATE/PROV.: _____ POSTAL/ZIP CODE: _____

Send your name and address, along with your cash register
receipts for proofs of purchase, to:

In the U.S.	In Canada
Harlequin Books	Harlequin Books
P.O. Box 9057	P.O. Box 622
Buffalo, NY	Fort Erie, Ontario
14269	L2A 5X3

PHQ4982

Take 2 bestselling love stories FREE

Plus get a FREE surprise gift!

Special Limited-Time Offer

Mail to Harlequin Reader Service®

3010 Walden Avenue
P.O. Box 1867
Buffalo, N.Y. 14240-1867

YES! Please send me 2 free Harlequin Romance® novels and my free surprise gift. Then send me 6 brand-new novels every month, which I will receive months before they appear in bookstores. Bill me at the low price of $2.90 each plus 25¢ delivery and applicable sales tax if any*. That's the complete price, and a saving of over 10% off the cover prices—quite a bargain! I understand that accepting the books and gift places me under no obligation ever to buy any books. I can always return a shipment and cancel at any time. Even if I never buy another book from Harlequin, the 2 free books and the surprise gift are mine to keep forever.

116 HEN CH66

Name	(PLEASE PRINT)
Address	Apt. No.
City	State	Zip

This offer is limited to one order per household and not valid to present Harlequin Romance® subscribers. *Terms and prices are subject to change without notice. Sales tax applicable in N.Y.

UROM-98

©1990 Harlequin Enterprises Limited

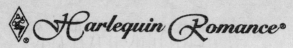

Invites You to A Wedding!

Whirlwind Weddings
Combines the heady romance of a whirlwind courtship with the excitement of a wedding—strong heroes, feisty heroines and marriages made not so much in heaven as in a hurry!

Some people say you can't hurry love—well, starting in August, look out for another selection of fabulous romances that prove that sometimes you can!

THE MILLION-DOLLAR MARRIAGE by Eva Rutland—
August 1998

BRIDE BY DAY by Rebecca Winters—
September 1998

READY-MADE BRIDE by Janelle Denison—
December 1998

Who says you can't hurry love?

Available wherever Harlequin books are sold.

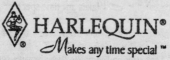

CHRISTMAS *Treats*

PENNY JORDAN,

DAY LECLAIRE &
LINDSAY ARMSTRONG

bring you the best of Christmas romance
in this wonderful holiday collection where
friends and family gather to celebrate
the holidays and make romantic wishes
come true.

Christmas Treats is available in November 1998,
at your favorite retail store.

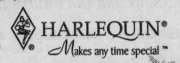

HARLEQUIN®
Makes any time special ™

If you're looking for more titles by
BETTY NEELS

Order now to receive more romantic stories
by one of Harlequin's most loved authors:

Harlequin Romance®

#03400	WAITING FOR DEBORAH	$3.25 U.S. ☐ $3.75 CAN. ☐
#03483	THE MISTLETOE KISS	$3.25 U.S. ☐ $3.75 CAN. ☐
#03492	MARRYING MARY	$3.50 U.S. ☐ $3.99 CAN. ☐
#03512	A KISS FOR JULIE	$3.50 U.S. ☐ $3.99 CAN. ☐

(limited quantities available on certain titles)

TOTAL AMOUNT	$
POSTAGE & HANDLING	$
($1.00 for one book, 50¢ for each additional)	
APPLICABLE TAXES*	$_____
TOTAL PAYABLE	$_____
(check or money order—please do not send cash)	

To order, complete this form and send it, along with a check or money order
for the total above, payable to Harlequin Books, to: **In the U.S.:** 3010 Walden
Avenue, P.O. Box 9047, Buffalo, NY 14269-9047; **In Canada:** P.O. Box 613,
Fort Erie, Ontario, L2A 5X3.

Name: _____

Address: _____ City: _____

State/Prov.: _____ Zip/Postal Code: _____

Account #: _____ 075CSAS

*New York residents remit applicable sales taxes.
 Canadian residents remit applicable GST and provincial taxes.

HARLEQUIN®
Makes any time special ™

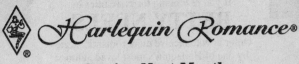

Harlequin Romance ®

Coming Next Month

Especially for Christmas we bring you a whole feast of delights.

#3531 READY-MADE BRIDE Janelle Denison

Andrew Fielding wants a mom and his daddy could use a wife. He thinks he's found the perfect woman for both of them: Megan Sanders. Which is fine with Megan—the Fielding men have their attractions: one's as cute as a button, the other very sexy and, together, they're the family Megan's always wanted! But convincing brooding widower Kane Fielding is less easy....

Whirlwind Weddings—*Who says you can't hurry love?*

#3532 GABRIEL'S MISSION Margaret Way

The way Chloe taunted her boss, Gabriel McGuire, at work could be amusing, but her reckless actions could also be downright exasperating! One of these days she'd take one risk too many. She'd probably worn out a whole host of guardian angels, but some small voice kept telling Gabriel that someone had to protect her and that *he* was the man for the job....

Guardian Angels—*Falling in love sometimes needs a little help from above!*

#3533 ONE NIGHT BEFORE CHRISTMAS Catherine Leigh

When Carly meets Jonah St. John at a Christmas party she decides that all she wants for Christmas this year is the tall, handsome tycoon... gift wrapped! And her wish comes true—at least temporarily. But then Carly learns that Santa's brought her a little something extra this year.... She's having Jonah's baby!

#3534 SANTA'S SPECIAL DELIVERY Val Daniels

Alicia believes that her handsome husband, Daniel, has only married her for their baby's sake, and that he is really in love with another woman. In fact Daniel *is* in love with Alicia, and wants their marriage to last forever—but will he be able to convince her before it's too late...?

Baby Boom—*Because two's company and three (or four or five) is a family!*